FOG OVER FUNDY

FOG OVER FUNDY

BY
LOUIS ARTHUR CUNNINGHAM

INTRODUCTION BY
GWENDOLYN DAVIES

© 2006 Formac Publishing Company Limited
Introduction © Gwendolyn Davies 2006

All rights reserved. No part of this book may be reproduced or transmitted in any form or by any means, electronic or mechanical, including photocopying, or by any information storage or retrieval system, without permission in writing from the publisher.

Formac Publishing Company Limited recognizes the support of the Province of Nova Scotia through the Department of Tourism, Culture and Heritage. We acknowledge the financial support of the Government of Canada through the Book Publishing Industry Development Program (BPIDP) for our publishing activities. We acknowledge the support of the Canada Council for the Arts for our publishing program.

Author's photo: Archives and Special Collections, Harriet Irving Library, University of New Brunswick

Library and Archives Canada Cataloguing in Publication

Cunningham, Louis Arthur, 1900-1954.
    Fog over Fundy / Louis Arthur Cunningham ; introduction by Gwendolyn Davies.

(Formac fiction treasures)
Reprint. First published: Philadelphia : Penn Pub. Co., 1936.
ISBN-10: 0-88780-710-0   ISBN-13: 978-0-88780-710-7

    1. Canadians, French-speaking—New Brunswick—Tantramar River Region—Fiction. I. Title. II. Series.

PS8505.U59F63 2006   C813'.52   C2006-904372-8

Series editor: Gwendolyn Davies

Formac Publishing Company Limited
5502 Atlantic Street
Halifax, Nova Scotia
B3H 1G4
www.formac.ca

Printed and bound in Canada

Presenting Formac Fiction Treasures
Series Editor: Gwendolyn Davies

A taste for reading popular fiction expanded in the nineteenth century with the mass marketing of books and magazines. People read rousing adventure stories aloud at night around the fireside; they bought entertaining romances to read while travelling on trains and curled up with the latest serial novel in their leisure moments. Novelists were important cultural figures, with devotees who eagerly awaited their next work.

Among the many successful popular English language novelists of the late 19th and early 20th centuries were a group of Maritimers who found in their own education, travel and sense of history, events and characters capable of entertaining readers on both sides of the Atlantic. They emerged from well-established communities that valued education and culture, for women as well as men. Faced with limited publishing opportunities, in the Maritimes, successful writers sought magazine and book publishers in the major cultural centres: New York, Boston, Philadelphia, London and sometimes Montreal and Toronto. They often enjoyed much success with readers at home, but the best of these writers found large audiences across Canada and in the United States and Great Britain.

The Formac Fiction Treasures series is aimed at offering contemporary readers access to books that were successful, often huge bestsellers in their time, but which are now little-known and often hard to find. The authors and titles selected are chosen first of all as enjoyable to read, and secondly for the light they shine on historical events and on attitudes and views of the culture from which they emerged. These complete original texts reflect values that are sometimes in conflict with those of today: for example, racism is often evident, and bluntly expressed. This collection of novels is offered as a step towards rediscovering a surprisingly diverse and not nearly well enough known popular cultural heritage of the Maritime provinces and of Canada.

Louis Arthur Cunningham

INTRODUCTION

Reading Louis Arthur Cunningham's 1936 novel *Fog Over Fundy* is a bit like being plunged into a late-1930s movie. There is a beautiful ash-blonde heroine of titled descent named Armande de Vysart. There is a disintegrating turreted family estate called "Beausejour" to which she has dedicated her life. There are three handsome suitors — one rich and powerful, one worthy and unexciting, and one dark and mysterious. And there is a mysterious death that fractures the de Vysart world, threatening to destroy the fragile happiness that beckons on the horizon for Armande.

But to reduce the novel to such filmlike simplicity is to ignore its other facets. For *Fog Over Fundy* emanated from the pen of one of New Brunswick's most prolific and inventive storywriters in the period between 1927 and 1954. And invariably, Louis Arthur Cunningham brought to his romances an understanding of the social and physical landscape of his native province. That he appropriated what was imaginatively useful to his fiction — ignoring or transforming what was not — occasionally drew him into controversy. But this is the challenge of the storyteller, and like Thomas Hardy with his tales of Wessex or Margaret Laurence with her interpretations of Manawaka, he selectively borrowed and shaped a fictional literary world from his region.

Thus, the community surrounding St. Bruno's church, five miles from the estate of Beausejour in *Fog Over Fundy*, for example, bears little physical resemblance to Memramcook in southeast New Brunswick as we know it today. But references to nearby Dorchester, Sackville, Pré d'en Haut, "the crossroads," the dikes, the aboideaux, the covered bridge (which once connected Upper Dorchester to Taylor Village) and the Tantramar marshes fix the landscape of the novel in a recognizable visual framework.

Nonetheless, Cunningham's St. Bruno — with its church, graveyard, White Roe Inn, printing office, five-mile clay road leading to Beausejour, fishing boats and tumbledown wharves — is an imaginative composite that he had to create for the physical working out of his story. He needed the bay to be nearby so that John Gower, the mysterious stranger, could survive a shipwreck and come into the lives of the villagers without explanation or background. He needed a traditional stone church with a fine organ, stained glass windows and a dramatic background as a venue for Armande's secret assignations with the mysterious stranger. And he needed the White Roe Inn (oddly named for an Acadian village) as a drinking place for the old men who generate the gossip that nearly kills Gower, Armande and their love.

Thus, literally, there is more than one "Fog over Fundy" in Cunningham's novel. On a physical level, the author paints a landscape of vast marshes on the edge of New Brunswick's Bay of Fundy. As Roger Lavergne, millionaire and persistent suitor for Armande's affections, tries to draw her away to the sophisticated delights of Montreal and Paris, she asserts her affiliation for her regional home: "Not for me ... here I have my roots and my being. Keep your Japanese gardens at the Ritz, your promenades on Dufferin Terrace and your skijoring at Lucerne — give me the dikes and the marshes and the sea and the wild geese winging north." It is appropriate that the reader's first introduction to Armande is of her riding hellbent on her horse through a stormy autumn night, hearing "the thunder of the tremendous waters of the Bay of Fundy as wave upon white-capped wave, tumbling, foaming, jostling like mad, hurled themselves against the mighty ramparts of the dike."

And when a fog of grief overwhelms her after the sensational New York killing of her beloved brother Leon, it is to the marshes, the dikes and the bay that she turns long after midnight, searching in the mystery of the stars and the sea for the spiritual consolation that only their vast grandeur can bring her. She could not, she thinks later as she sits in the old stone church, "be uprooted from this soil, this land, of which she was a part — never uprooted to be taken away, to fade, to wither, to die in some place beyond sight and sound of the things she loved so warmly."

Both the physical fog over the Tantramar and Armande's fog of grief become intermingled with a third kind of fog in the novel. This is the fog of misunderstanding and mystery that surrounds the death of Leon de Vysart, supposedly at the hand of a missing New Yorker, Michael Dumont. That Dumont is linked to the mysterious stranger, John Gower; that Armande hides a terrible secret; and that the villagers read into their romance the union of the devil and his witch only serve to thicken this fog, and becomes an escalating nightmare for the protagonists as the novel moves to its conclusion. Facing a revengeful mob from the steps of the grey stone church, with its high cross dark against the sky, Armande becomes Cunningham's sacrificial Christ figure crying to her persecutors before the crucifix: "You do not know what you are doing." Chunks of ice rain around her, rough hands seize her, and she is pulled to the ground by those who tear at her garments. It is this fog — the fog of fear, ignorance and violence — that Cunningham dramatically develops in the novel. And in the end, when his protagonists survive to love and forgive, they do so not only in the context of divine grace but also in a belief in the spirituality of the land.

Even before the publication of *Fog Over Fundy*, Cunningham had established his credentials as a theatrical and regionally focused writer. Born in Saint John, New Brunswick, in 1900, he received his B.A. and his M.A. from St. Joseph's College in Memramcook, New Brunswick. There he studied French, English and Latin, but he also absorbed from his association with rural Acadians and his proximity to the physical landscape of the Bay of Fundy those elements that were to inform a number of his short stories and novels. Thus, it is not surprising that his first novel, *Yvon Tremblay*, was set in the Memramcook Valley. The area "rivals in beauty, quaintness, and wealth of purely rustic types the Wessex country of Thomas Hardy's immortal novels," he told a Saint John newspaper in 1927, just before the book was published by Graphic Press in Ottawa, and he clearly felt that he had not exhausted what he called the "Tantramar" landscape when he turned to the writing of *Fog Over Fundy* nine years later.

Between the writing of the two novels, however, Cunningham had begun to build a reputation as an author of both short and long fiction. Having left his academic studies and teaching at the Catholic University of America and at Notre Dame University well behind him, he eventually settled with his wife in Hammond River, New Brunswick, where he wrote in a large, bright, comfortable room with high windows. In an interview in the Saint John *Evening Times-Globe* in October 1961, his wife recalled that he worked at a large oak desk, seated in a regular office chair. His room also contained an old-fashioned rocking chair, a studio couch and two bookcases. His favourite novelists, whom he read avidly when not writing, included Fielding, Richardson, Dickens, Thackeray, Stevenson and Hardy. He deeply admired *The Golden Dog* by Canadian novelist William Kirby, defying anyone, he told a reporter in 1927, "to produce a better historical novel."

And as readers of *Fog Over Fundy* can infer, he was a great admirer of First World War poet Rupert Brooke, whose lines leap to the lips of Armande, Marc Duclos and John Gower in this novel. Although Canada was inexorably leading up to a second war in 1936, when *Fog Over Fundy* was published, the reader is never far from references to the lingering physical and spiritual wounds of the earlier conflict in the 1920s — the period in which the novel is set. Armande's brother, Leon, had gone to war at the age of 17, "red-headed and wild as a hare." He returned, she mourns, with that boy "forever gone beyond recalling." In his place was "a hard man with steel-blue eyes, with a hard deep-lined mouth and the mien of an eagle fretted with the earth." He had become, in the famous words of Gertrude Stein, yet another member of the "lost generation" of the 1920s, restlessly roaming the world — in his case, to fly for hire wherever there was a war.

His death in a hunting lodge after a shallow acquaintanceship with a New York showgirl makes him seem like yet another delayed victim of the war, a man who, in the words of Ulric de Vysart, "lived with Death ... walked with it, flew with it, slept with it," and held it "in fine contempt." Yet after Leon's demise, Armande preserves his room — "a lovely room," as his son, young Paul Emil, sees it, with "guns and soldiers' hats and pictures of great airships, and silver cups and many books and a hundred other things." And Armande begins to create her brother's mythology for the son he never knew and for the continuation of the de Vysart dynasty. "He flew in those airships you saw. He was in many wars. He was strong," she tells him.

Once launched on his career as novelist and short-story writer, Cunningham continued to weave into his stories a blend of regional New Brunswick landscapes, local history and contemporary themes. His 1929 modernist novel, *This Thing Called Love* — quixotically titled after a Cole Porter song issued earlier that same year — was edgy Canadian fiction for its time. According to an article on Cunningham in the *Toronto Daily Star* in June 1939, it "roused a storm in staid old St. John," presumably because it focused, in spite of its understated style, on the protagonist's growing obsession with the social outcast Esther Pym (her name evoking comparisons with Nathaniel Hawthorne's sexual outcast, Hester Prynne in *The Scarlet Letter*). As the Toronto *Mail and Empire* noted in a review in June 1929, the unique feature of the novel is not that Graham Starr is caught in a relationship with a "nice" girl while being obsessed with a "member of the ancient profession," but that Starr and Pym meet only once in the novel. Yet as the reviewer points out, "the tie between them is the most vital human relation in the book," particularly as Esther emerges from the novel as a "reproach" to "the conventionally good people of our time and country."

This Thing Called Love was published in the same era as Morley Callaghan's *Strange Fugitive*, Ernest Hemingway's

A Farewell to Arms, and F. Scott Fitzgerald's *The Great Gatsby*. It was an exciting time for the novel, but, as Cunningham made clear in interviews, the need to keep bread upon the table left him little opportunity to hone the "cool, chaste skill" for which the *Mail and Empire* praised him in 1929. Interviewed by Douglas A. MacLennan in the *Toronto Daily Star* in June 1939, just three years after the publication of *Fog Over Fundy*, Cunningham revealed that he wrote compulsively, banning the radio, telephone and doorbell from his home so that he could have total solitude in which to work. Once embarked on a story or novel, he composed furiously in longhand, and his wife then typed the manuscript. He never read over his text, never changed the plot once he had started to write and ate and slept just enough to finish "thousands of words a day" until the story was ready for final revision. By Christmas of that year, he told the reporter, he would have completed and sold six book-length novels and 150,000 words of short stories and articles to magazines.

The magazines to which Cunningham contributed included such Canadian household names as the *Canadian Magazine*, *Chatelaine*, *Canadian Home* and *The Star Weekly*. He also sold successfully to American and British publications, the British market becoming particularly important to him in the Second World War years when, according to an *Evening Times-Globe* story about him in October 1961, "I could not have survived the last few years — that is, kept my place and my life pretty much intact — had it not been for the steadiness, reliability and consistency of the English magazine market. Not once did that market turn down a good story; not once did it fail to pay; not once did it make a bad grimace or cry havoc."

Like many writers, Cunningham also hoped that Hollywood would discover him, an aspiration realized in 1942 when 20th Century Fox bought his novel *The Princess of Gratzen* for transfer to the screen. Saint John, which had been unhappy about *This Thing Called Love*, now heralded his Hollywood accomplishment in tones usually reserved for native son Walter Pidgeon, who had starred in the 1941 Oscar-winning *How Green Was My Valley*, and who was the male lead in the 1942 Oscar-nominated *Mrs. Miniver*. The local by-line, "Novel By Cunningham to Become Hollywood Feature Production" and "Another Name Added to Saint John Group in Spotlight," must have been gratifying to Cunningham, who regularly drove the 18 miles from his home at Hammond River to the city in his large yellow roadster, a car closely approximating the one driven by F. Scott Fitzgerald's high-flying Jay Gatsby in the novel and film *The Great Gatsby*. To this day, Saint John folklore recalls Cunningham driving his convertible touring car through the streets of the city's south end in the late 1930s and 1940s, and at least one of Cunningham's Toronto visitors commented on Cunningham's "motoring at break-neck speed along country roads, dust swirling about him." Surviving letters at the University of New Brunswick reveal that, when not writing, Cunningham and his wife frequently took to the road for recreation to escape the wearying regimen of composition.

By the time he had reached the age of 50, Cunningham had published more than 15 novels and hundreds of short stories. Ruminating on the significance of this landmark birthday in September 1950, he noted that "I enjoy everything — and I mean everything — far more than of old perhaps because as time grows short I learn to nurse my pleasures and value them more; perhaps it is that, like good liquor and good cheddar, I have mellowed with the years." He noted with regret the passing of friends, and even the razing of his old school in Saint John brought a reaction "something like bewilderment." Yet he continued to write actively, producing at least 11 more novels before he died of a heart attack at the age of 53.

A letter written by his wife after Cunningham's death indicates that she continued to sell his unpublished fiction: she had to, as "Art" had not carried insurance. At least seven more novels were published after his death, and Hortense Cunningham's correspondence reveals that she was receiving between $150 and $250 for each of his unpublished stories in 1954. "Money never meant anything to us," she adds in her letter. "We spent as we earned and I am sure we both had no regrets. We had a very happy and contented life. I have not a sorry moment to remember."

Louis Arthur Cunningham's obituary in the Saint John *Telegraph-Journal* on June 14, 1954, noted that his short stories and articles had been published in more than 100 magazines in Canada, the United States, Britain, Australia, Denmark and Java. That he had cultivated such a broad international readership while continuing to know and love Acadian traditions speaks volumes of his ability to tell a good story with universal appeal. The original reviews of *Fog Over Fundy* in 1936 reflect that appeal, with *Books* commenting on Cunningham's "talent for incisive prose" and the *Boston Transcript* on his "high sense of romance" and "atmosphere of other-worldliness." Most reviews invariably complimented Cunningham on his ability to evoke a sense of region, with *Books* emphasizing his "wild setting," the *Boston Transcript* his "delightful folk," and the *New York Times* (Dec. 6, 1936) his "considerable effective scenic description." Thus, although it was clear to Canadian readers who knew Acadian social patterns that Cunningham's interpretation of Acadian regional culture was often highly selective, it is also clear that he was capable of evocatively conveying to international readers a visual and auditory sense of the Memramcook region that he loved. Examples from *Fog Over Fundy* abound. The reader can vividly identify with Armande and Gower as they walk together in the moonlight "past the sleeping farmsteads, greeted now and then by the echoing bark, clear in the night, of some wakeful collie." It is Cunningham's invocation of the modifier "wakeful," and his precision in identifying the breed of barking dog, that turns a mundane image into a vivid, imagined moment. Elsewhere the reader can almost feel the icy winter storm: "Late in the evening the snow ceased and the wind abated; the stars shone out like small, bright spear-points, hard, cruel, metallic. The frost-tortured trees in the park cracked with the sharp, staccato sounds of rifle fire and the bitter cold against one's face was a concrete, a tangible thing." And the reader can savour the quick-wittedness of Cunningham's assessment of a lanky, local poet in the White Roe Inn as "this Ichabod Crane of the marshes." It is this talent for what *Books* called Cunningham's "incisive prose" that brought Cunningham's New Brunswick-specific tales to life and gave them universal appeal.

Today, Louis Arthur Cunningham is no longer a household name. *Fog Over Fundy*, which began as a serialized novel in the *Canadian Home Journal* in September 1936, was submitted to the Penn Publishing Company of Philadelphia for publication in November, 1936, and was reprinted by Penn in 1940. It has long been out of print. It is therefore exciting that this novel will once again be available through the *Formac Fiction Treasures* series.

New readers are invited to suspend their twenty-first century preoccupations and think back to the movie culture of the late thirties. Armande de Vysart is not quite Scarlett O'Hara in *Gone With the Wind*. But like Scarlett, she is a beautiful, reckless young woman, who discovers that at the core of her being lies her love of the land, her love of her family name, her love of her penniless family estate and her love of a man whom society does not condone. Armande's spiritual growth through loneliness, community ostracization and an atypical romance demonstrate the writing talent that once made Louis Arthur Cunningham one of Maritime Canada's best-known ambassadors of the popular novel.

                        Gwendolyn Davies, Ph.D., FRSC
                        University of New Brunswick

GWENDOLYN DAVIES is Dean of Graduate Studies and Associate Vice President, Research at the University of New Brunswick. A member of the university's English department, she has spoken and published widely on Atlantic literature. She is a member of the Royal Society of Canada.

> *" How e'er it be, it seems to me,*
> *'Tis only noble to be good:*
> *Kind hearts are more than coronets*
> *And simple faith than Norman blood"*
>
> TENNYSON

CONTENTS

I. THE FACE OF THE DROWNED	9
II. BEAUSEJOUR	37
III. LITANY	64
IV. MISERERE	92
V. THE WITCH AND THE PEASANT	120
VI. THE FIRST SNOW	149
VII. PAUL EMIL	181
VIII. THREE WHO LOVED HER	219
IX. AT THE WHITE ROE	253
X. LIGHT WHERE WAS DARKNESS	285

FOG OVER FUNDY

CHAPTER I

THE FACE OF THE DROWNED

IT rained, as only in Ultima Thule it can rain — a driving, hissing, lashing rain that turned the red clay of the marsh road into a viscous liquid, that sent up countless angry little geysers from the ponds and the roadside ditches, that tore the fast fading leaves from their weakened hold on the willow branches, that did fiendish work everywhere, this Autumn twilight, save where it beaded and jewelled in the ash-gold hair of Armande de Vysart, who rode her black mare Feu Follet along the road that runs in the shelter of the great dike and carries such few as seek these remote regions of the Tantramar to the village of St. Bruno.

Armande heard, like the bourdon of a million contra-basses, the thunder of the tremendous waters of the

FOG OVER FUNDY

Bay of Fundy as wave upon white-capped wave, tumbling, foaming, jostling like mad, hurled themselves against the mighty ramparts of the dike. The rain dripped from her sodden brown felt, ran in streams from the fawn Burberry that wisely she had carried when at four o'clock she had started on this solitary ride.

Past six now and the grayness of the last light turning into black. "And still five miles, *mon vieux*, to Beausejour," said Armande to the weary Feu Follet. " And the mud makes heavy going and you, more than I, *chérie*, are weary and wet. Well then, we shall stop at the inn of Isaac Proux and I shall telephone to Ulric to send for me and you shall sleep this night in the stables of the White Roe. Understood? "

It seemed to be. Feu Follet trotted briskly but carefully over the slippery rutted road. A half-mile further along there was a cross-roads and a tall sign-post like a gibbet stood starkly out of the gloom; hardby lights glimmered, warm and ruddy, and the bitter pungent tang of wood-smoke, driven groundward by the wild east wind, tickled Armande's nostrils. Feu Follet, un-

THE FACE OF THE DROWNED

bidden, turned in at stone gate-posts set in a row of pollard-willows, and whinnied shrilly in answer to salutations from Isaac Proux's Percherons in the great stable behind the inn.

A dwarfish figure, a coat worn cape-fashion over his shoulders, with head bent against the wind and rain, darted from the porch of the White Roe and took Feu Follet's head as Armande dismounted.

"A bitter night, ma'm'selle," said a broad Breton voice. "You do well to stop. One says the dike is all but burst at Pré des Capucins."

"So? I am glad to know it. I only stop here to wait for my brother to send a car. It can come by Pré d'en haut. Feu Follet, however, will be an overnight guest, Gil. See to her well, *hein?* "

"Certainly, ma'm'selle."

Squat Gil d'Entremont led the steaming mare to the dry straw and warmth of the stable. Armande passed under the dim light of an old ship's lantern that hung creaking above the low door, into the goodly warmth of the inn. Isaac Proux, who had known three generations of de Vysarts, and who, no doubt at all, had looked

FOG OVER FUNDY

precisely the same to Armande's grand-father St. Just, hurried forward, bowing deeply, to greet her. He was thin and cadaverous, was Isaac Proux, and sallow and pockmarked and where one eye should be was a black patch and the other seemed red in the light of the lamps and the roaring fire.

"Place for an orphan of the storm, Boniface," laughed Armande, shrugging out of the sodden Burberry, drawing off the long gauntlets and perching the brown felt with its forlorn little feather on the newel of the banister where dark stairs led above.

"Place always for one of your name, Ma'm'selle Armande," said Isaac Proux. He clapped his hands. "I shall have Elodie light the fire in the big room for you. I shall have a repast ready in a few moments."

Armande nodded. She walked, tall, long-legged, exquisitely slender of waist and shoulder, over to the hearth where some old men were sitting. She bowed to their salutations. She stood, hands outstretched to the grateful heat. The warm light flickered on her face framed by the thick ashen tresses, by the high neck of a yellow sweater and the collar of a brown tweed jacket.

THE FACE OF THE DROWNED

Her eyes were blue, her skin smooth, flushed with rose-pink, her mouth wide, firm, with short upper lip; a Norman face, the nose small with tiny arched nostrils, the chin strong and slightly pointed. The old men, three of them, all long past the days of toil, watched her covertly and did not speak. No doubt one or all of them had seen other de Vysarts stand thus, hands in pockets, long legs spread, and gaze into the flamy caverns of a hearth with that far off, dreamy look in their eyes. Mad — some said they were mad. Sure, they did strange things. This slip of a girl, for instance, barely nineteen, riding through an Autumn gale that kept stout men by the fireside, wandering solitary over the marshes, equally at home in a palace or a peasant's cottage; so fine, yet so much like themselves. No better judge of hound or horse, they knew, in all the Acadian land. Here today; tomorrow one might read in la Patrie or la Presse that she was at the Ritz or the Manoir Richelieu or even on her way to London.

Absently she fished a loose cigarette from her pocket and lighted it. She looked at the grizzled, granite faces.

FOG OVER FUNDY

"How is your good wife, Floribert? Better of the rheumatism?"

"Somewhat better, Ma'm'selle de Vysart, thank you."

"And your son Paul, Jean Belliveau — he has been discharged from the Military Hospital?"

"Yes, ma'm'selle. He is home now. He coughs."

"It was cruel, the war. You will excuse me. I must telephone to my brother."

Armande strolled to the hall and cranked the obsolete contraption that was the pride of the White Roe. But no voice came and only the fury of the storm sang to her remotely over the wires. Isaac came as she waited, and said regretfully, "I fear it is no use: the wires are down in many places. It is, without doubt, the worst storm in many years. Mark me, some of the dikes will go out tonight. There is no dike strong enough to stand such terrible assaults of wind and sea."

Armande shrugged. "Always it abates, Isaac, and the sun shines out and the world seems the better of its purging. I shall go up to my room now. It is the one at the stair-head?"

THE FACE OF THE DROWNED

"I shall conduct you."

"No need for it, my friend."

She went upstairs, her youth, her beauty seeming so incongruous in this old place; seeming, yet, to shed such freshness and radiance that Isaac Proux, watching from the stair-foot, felt glad. Farmers and their wives on market days, and lorry drivers and the like were all that the White Roe was accustomed to shower its hospitality upon. Other de Vysarts had come there in the six decades of Isaac Proux's memory — but none so fair as this girl, the youngest of her house.

Truly none so fair. Candles burned in silver sconces on either side of the mirror atop the old rosewood dresser in the big room at the stair-head. Gently their yellow light shone upon her face, and could the high-necked sweater have given way to a low cut dress and the close waves of her wondrous blonde hair to curls and ringlets, the centuries would have dropped away and a flower than which no fairer ever bloomed in the court of *le grand monarque* would have stood this bitter Autumn night in the little inn on the farthest reaches of the Tantramar.

FOG OVER FUNDY

She washed hands and face in the great basin in the alcove, combed out the thick tresses and re-arranged them. On a little table by the hearth there was food set out and a small decanter. Elodie, Isaac Proux's niece, a dark quiet girl, came with hot coffee and some *poutine râpée,* an Acadian dish, a pudding of rare succulence, and there were eggs and honey. Armande lingered a while with her coffee and cigarette. Outside the sturdy windows the storm raged unabated, the faded creepers tapped the pane, the candles flickered in the draft, and all through the ancient house were strange murmurs and rustlings and creaking sounds. And she, who rarely knew what it was to be lonely, save in a crowd, felt loneliness here, and she spoke aloud, just to hear the sound of a human voice —

"I know how Mariana felt in her moated grange — this place is moated and beleaguered by the wind-demons and the rain and the sea and the marshlands where one would be lost forever on such a night as this —

'All day within the dreary house,
The doors upon their hinges creaked,

THE FACE OF THE DROWNED

The blue fly sung in the pane; the mouse
Behind the mouldering wainscot shriek'd
Or from the crevice peer'd about.
Old faces glimmer'd through the doors,
Old footsteps trod the upper floor,
Old voices called her from without.
She only said, 'My life is dreary
He cometh not,' she said;
She said, 'I am aweary, aweary.
I would that I were dead.'"

Armande stood up, shot the cigarette deftly into the hearth. She shivered; not with cold, not with fear; with some nameless, unknown thing. The warm room, the fire, the clean smelling bed and the snowy pillows had no attraction for her now. She went to the window and pressed her face against the streaming pane. Perhaps out there, out in that maelstrom of wind and rain, it would be nicer than in here. One fled from things. One knew no reason for fleeing. Sometimes happiness dwelt in the strangest places, at the strangest times: on a hilltop at dawn with the sun rising in a fantastic fanfare of

FOG OVER FUNDY

golden trumpets behind a palisade of white young birches, on a rocky promontory when the sea surged gray and sullen and the buoys clanged dismally out of the mist and the water snarled among the sharp cruel rocks at one's feet. And one could be so utterly miserable and forlorn in places where men spent money like water to make mirth.

Abruptly she turned from the window and left the room. She walked softly downstairs, walked down out of the shadows into the genial brightness. The old men still sat, waiting out the storm, and Isaac Proux sat with them and they drank rum. She could smell its pungence and the cloves mingled with it. Martin Theriault, the most ancient of the three was talking in a low voice that, at times, the tempest's furious onslaughts against door and shutter all but drowned.

"— on nights like this that Damase Blais, who for many years was dikemaster in these regions, comes back and presses his drowned face against the window panes and turns men's hearts to stone—" The old man's voice was deep, vibrant with his belief in this ancient tale.

THE FACE OF THE DROWNED

The girl Elodie, standing beside her uncle, glanced timidly at the window and screamed and covered her eyes with her apron. Isaac Proux jumped up, overturning his chair with a great crash. The old men's jaws sagged down, their eyes, terror-filled, were glued on the low window by the door, upon the white visage that looked like the face of the drowned. Fingers like dead fingers tapped the pane. Armande took the three bottom steps as one, and ran to the door. Isaac followed. Together they raised the man sprawled upon the porch, carried him into the inn and laid him on a settle by the hearth.

"*Mon Dieu*," said Isaac, crossing himself, "he frightened me."

"Let us have some brandy, Isaac." Armande touched the white cold brow, felt the faint pulse-beat at the temple. He was a young man, dark, slender. He wore a seaman's reefer, which they removed. There was a bit of a gash in the side of his head and the bright blood glared in contrast out of his pallor. The girl Elodie, quite recovered, went away and returned, very quiet and efficient, with a basin of water, and towels and

FOG OVER FUNDY

clean cloth for bandages. Armande forced a little of the brandy that Isaac brought, between the stranger's lips. He stirred and groaned but did not regain consciousness. With Elodie's help, she bathed and dressed his wound; then Isaac and the old men carried him to the bedroom off the inn-parlor and undressed him and left him there.

Isaac looked through the pockets of the reefer. A pipe, an oilskin tobacco-pouch, sodden matches, a knife, odds-and-ends such as men ever accumulate. From the inside pocket the inn-keeper fished a wallet fastened with a rubber-band. He opened this.

"Here is his name," he announced. "It says, 'John Gower, Far Rockaway, New York. Seaman aboard Yacht Triton. Owner, David Loring, Jr., New York.'" Isaac looked from the old men to Elodie to Armande de Vysart. "He came, then, from the sea."

"No doubt he came from this yacht," said Armande. "They must have been foolhardy people to sail in these waters in such a storm. If he got ashore from her and made his way here, it is a wonder; if anyone else did, it

THE FACE OF THE DROWNED

is a miracle. He seems to be very ill. He should have a doctor."

"But this night, one could not—" Isaac Proux faltered. Armande was smiling. He had seen others of that ilk smile even so. Again he would have crossed himself before what he saw in her eyes, but he could not lift his hand to his brow.

"I shall go to St. Bruno and bring the doctor."

"But— but the roads — the broken dikes—"

"I think he has broken ribs. Tell Gil d'Entremont to saddle Feu Follet. You know, good Isaac, Feu Follet is the Will o' the Wisp and she knows the moors in darkness deeper than this. She was weary, which was why I let her rest. Now she shall take me to St. Bruno. I shall return with Marc Duclos, who will minister to this bit of jetsam."

The inn-keeper protested no further. It was useless, he knew. She wanted to go out into the storm, into the howling wind and the sheeted rain. There was something out there in the murk of the marshes that called to her, something wild and fearful that found an echo in her wild spirit. She donned her riding coat, belted and

FOG OVER FUNDY

strapped it, she crushed her hat over her pale hair and drew on her gloves. She smiled at the silent watchers and bowed gravely. " Aurevoir. I shall soon return."

" God go with you," murmured Isaac Proux. Gil d' Entremont's lantern glimmered wan outside the window and the mare's hoofs clicked on the cobbles. With a wave of gauntletted hand, Armande breasted the wind and strode across the inn-porch. She said something at once sharp and caressing to the great mare, as she mounted. In a moment, like a phantom, she had gone, swallowed up in the howling fugues of the gale.

Isaac Proux went on tiptoe to the room off the parlor and gazed upon the man who lay there in troubled sleep. He breathed though, it seemed, a whit easier; but he was not well; without a doctor he might die.

" Even," said Isaac, " for a lame dog that one would go through hell, yet like the others she can be cruel — to herself. May the good God calm that wild heart of hers and St. Bruno pray for her."

She needed such guidance and such prayers. Through darkness blacker than the pit, over roads that were now

THE FACE OF THE DROWNED

a quagmire, now a long lake, she rode, head down, shouting with reckless gallantry to the mare, now chiding her for being an old woman afraid of a little rain, now singing a rollicking folk-song to encourage her. The great dike held strong, not in the memory of man had it ever burst, not since that long ago time of which old Martin Theriault had told this night in the inn-parlor, when Damase Blais the Dikemaster who was mad and wicked, had blown up the aboideau at Pré des Capucins in an effort to drown his enemy and destroy his lands — Damase Blais who, on nights of storm like this, still haunted with the dank sea weed glued to his awful face, the remote villages of the Tantramar and peered in cottage windows and presaged death by drowning.

"Some will drown tonight," mused Armande, who had been brought up on this tale and a hundred others like it. "And Damase will have enough victims to content him until Christmas at least. On, Feu Follet! What is a little water to you, *ma brave!*" The mare struggled out of a slough up to her saddle girth onto higher ground and trotted with splendid gallantry into the deserted straggling street of St. Bruno. In a few cottages lights burned. Dr. Marc Duclos was still awake. Armande could see him reading by his hearth-fire as she strode across the verandah and tapped with her riding-crop on the pane.

He came quickly and held the door with his foot from driving back against the wall. In the light of the porch lamp he stared at her. " The devil! " he said. " Come in. I beg your pardon. I was not — "

Laughing, she walked in. " Have your man stable my horse, Marc, and have him get out your car. We return to the White Roe at *le grand carrefour,* where a man lies very ill."

" You came from there! You rode through this just because some man is ill. Tell me are you goddess or devil or woman! You seem happy. I swear you have enjoyed this night of hell."

"I have laughed and I have sung. Come, Marc — hurry! We have detours to make."

Young Doctor Duclos looked at her for a moment with a mixture of helplessness and admiration. She had taken a cigarette from the howdah atop a silver ele-

THE FACE OF THE DROWNED

phant on his desk, and lighted it. She was looking at the fire. He went to find Néri Cormier, his man, and to prepare for the trip. All evening he had prayed that he might be permitted to rest by his fireside, but for Armande de Vysart one was glad to go.

"Who is this who is ill?" He came into the study belting his trench-coat. "Isaac Proux? Old Gil d'Entremont?"

"John Gower, seaman aboard the yacht Triton, native of Far Rockaway, New York."

"*Mon Dieu!* There has been a wreck then!"

"I fear so. He came from the sea. It was most strange, Marc. You know on such nights as this Damase Blais wanders along the dikes and presses his face against windows. *Bien!* I was just coming down the stairs of the White Roe and had stopped on the third step from the bottom to listen to old Martin Theriault relate how Damase Blais wandered accursed upon the earth, when I saw something white at the window-pane and then Elodie screamed and all but fainted — and there it was — the face of the drowned.

"Well, he lay unconscious on the porch when Isaac

FOG OVER FUNDY

and I got there. He had a gash in his head. We fixed it, gave him some brandy, undressed him and put him to bed. He did not recover consciousness. I thought it best to come fetch you. I know, of course, you would never want to sit by the fire while someone suffered even with the measles. You will enjoy the ride. We shall have to go by Pré d'en haut. Some of the dikes will have gone by now."

" Armande! Armande! " He shook his head. " Truly, you are fearfully and wonderfully made. How came you to be roaming about the Tantramar in this storm like a female Damase Blais, anyway? "

" Oh, just out riding. There's the car. Come — "

" Why do you not stay here, Armande? You must be tired — "

" I shall go with you. Tell your housekeeper, will you please, to call Beausejour and inform Ulric of my whereabouts. I do not feel like talking with Ulric tonight. By the time I do get home he should be in bed." She went out to the car. Marc Duclos called his message to the housekeeper, then got in beside Armande and the car sloshed away into the darkness, following

THE FACE OF THE DROWNED

warily the rain-striped pathway of its own making.

"Why should you go to so much trouble, even put your own life in danger, for this man?" demanded Marc.

"I should have done the same for anyone." But she thought, even as she spoke, "Would I? What was there about that man, about that dark face? Even while he lay there half dead there was something bitter and terribly sad about him and I fancied, if his eyes had opened, I'd have seen a bit of hell in them. Why, I wonder."

"You have been doing mad things since you wore pinafores, Armande — or did little girls wear pinafores so few years ago?"

Armande laughed. "I wore breeks as soon as I could talk the good Compte de Vysart into letting me have them and a pony to go with them. Mad things, you say, Marc? It depends much on one's viewpoint. What might seem utterly mad to you seems quite the natural thing for me. I see nothing in riding through a bit of wind and rain — " The car rocked with the blast — " to bring a doctor to an injured man."

FOG OVER FUNDY

"Madness!" growled Marc. "You might have been thrown from Feu Follet. You might have been drowned in a torrent or in the flood from a burst dike."

"I did not think of those dangers, my grave young doctor. I do not fear such things. You have read in Rupert Brooke—

'Naught broken save this body; lost but breath—'

It is the things that mutilate the spirit, Marc, and leave wounds that will not heal upon the heart, that Armande dreads. The body is such a poor thing, so perishable, so doomed to withering and decay — but the spirit shines with beauty and the heart pulses with such warm life. So these I would not risk, would not gamble; these I keep shut up in strong armor and defend with all the weapons that I know how to use."

"You think your armor and your weapons will always be adequate to protect you? Someday, something will be strong enough to beat down your Toledo blades and spike your guns and break your walls, *mignonne*, and then—you will be undone."

THE FACE OF THE DROWNED

"You have given up the assault, Marc."

He did not, for a while, answer. He gave her a cigarette, took one himself. His hand shook as he held the match, his eyes lingered on her face, pale, sweet as a tired flower. "I too dread the wound of the spirit more than that of the body. The one I know how to heal; the other —" He waved his cigarette in a glowing arc. It was very dark there. Néri had put out the dashlamps so better to utilize all the brightness of his beams.

"I did not wound your spirit, Marc. Say I did not."

"If I loved you and told you so, *chèrie,* and you could not love me — No, if these are wounds they are of my own inflicting. It was a dream, Armande, so fair and wondrous and so strong that its beauty lingers still. It started when I was a little boy going to school in St. Bruno. You did not know me then and I, of course, only saw you as you passed on horseback or in your father's big car. And you were from Beausejour, from a castle, and your father was the Compte de Vysart and you had great wealth. My home was a cottage, my people farmers, my station in life very humble. But I

FOG OVER FUNDY

had dreams such as a god might have and I was bold to hope —

"So I went through school and college and scholarships took me to Laval and to the Salpetrière and when I studied with the greatest men in France, I thanked you, for you had brought me there —"

"No, Marc! Please —"

"But yes. I am only a country doctor now, Armande, but for a while I was a god of your making."

Her mouth trembled. He did not see it there in the darkness. He did not hear the wail in her heart. He did not know how much she wanted to take him in her arms and press his dark head against the small, firm contours of her breast. "Why can't I? Why can't I? Surely he is fine and good and his love must be a splendid thing, that has persisted all these years despite my unkindness and often my ridicule, for I have tried to laugh him out of it. With never a kiss from me, never a caress —"

"You will find some better girl than I, Marc. I do not just say that because it seems the thing to say; I mean it. You are young. You say you are only a country doctor — what better thing could you be, you high

THE FACE OF THE DROWNED

priest of fevers and plagues and cuts and burns? What more can any doctor do than you do right here? And you know you love it. You know you did not mind turning out tonight — "

"It was for you."

"It was for one in pain. You would have done it for anyone."

"But more gladly for you, Armande. I — I would do anything for you, Armande. I would give my life, my soul, my chance of heaven for — " He stopped. "Forgive me. I know I am unfair to make you listen to such things."

"No. No. It is I who am unworthy to hear them from you. How slow Néri drives! I hope nothing has gone wrong with our patient. I did not like the look of him."

"No? He is ugly then."

Armande shrugged. "I did not mean that. You purposely misunderstand, Marc. I feared he might be more hurt than we could tell."

"One soon shall see."

FOG OVER FUNDY

Isaac Proux greeted them at the door of the White Roe as they dashed in out of the unceasing downpour. The three old men, bearded, gnarled, sage-looking as the magi of old, still sat by the fire, as much a part of the hearth, seemingly, as the great iron firedogs, the tongs, the bellows or the crane from which the black pot hung. Now and again, in the back-draft, pungent wood-smoke gusted into the room and mingled its fragrance with the acrid odor of native tobacco smoked in carven pipes of apple-wood.

"Still he sleeps, *m'sieur le docteur*," said Isaac. "I have gone there several times to his room to gaze upon him. He stirs sometimes and says one word."

"What does he say?" Armande de Vysart was again divesting herself of the sodden weather-proof, the hat and gauntlets; rain glistened on the fine tan leather of her boots. She asked the question idly enough, but her head jerked up and the blue eyes were wide when Isaac Proux said, "Candace."

"Candace?" Armande stared into Marc Duclos' quick brown eyes. "How strange!"

The doctor shrugged, spread his hands that had the

THE FACE OF THE DROWNED

strength of a peasant's, the fineness of a great surgeon's.
"Why strange? All men, I think, at one time or other in life, call a woman's name. Usually in time of agony or need. Take me to him, Isaac."

Armande went to the fire and stood there as before, gazing into the flames. The old men watched her covertly. Most of the time of her absence they had spent in talking of her family, the many de Vysarts, good and bad, who had lived at the big house called Beausejour; of Charleroi de Vysart who had come to worse than ruin through gaming and drink and women; of Alderic who had been drowned when recklessly he tried to swim his mount across a flood swollen river; of Simone the Fair who had shut herself up in the grim house when death claimed her lover and had never again gone forth until they took the faded flower of her beauty to the church of St. Bruno for its requiem; of this girl Armande who was, they believed, a witch, who rode at dead of night under the moon, who played the great organ in the church with only the straggling moonbeams colored by the stained glass window to light the choir-loft, who feared neither god nor man nor fire nor flood.

FOG OVER FUNDY

Armande gave no thought to the old men; only to that young one who had escaped by a miracle the sea-cold, clammy fingers of Damase Blais and had found succor in her arms. Candace — why did he say Candace? And did he call upon this unknown with reproach or with desire? What would one see in those eyes of his when they opened? Strangely he fascinated her, this bit of jetsam from another world, cast up on the lonely shores of the Tantramar. She walked slowly into the room, where lamps burned brightly, where Marc Duclos, his sleeves rolled up over strong forearms, knelt by the bed.

She came on tiptoe to the foot of the bed and even as she looked the stranger's eyes opened and stared into hers, for a moment blankly; then with terrible suddenness something sprang into them that frightened her, that made her step back quickly — she, Armande de Vysart, who feared neither god, man nor devil. But this, she knew, was hate — stark, awful — hate not for her but for some other whom the fevered brain saw in her beauty. When again she looked he still stared at her and he began to mutter incoherent things and tried to rise

THE FACE OF THE DROWNED

as if he would seize her and destroy her.

"Go, Armande," said Marc. "He is delirious. He mistakes you for some other."

She tore herself away from the madness in the stranger's eyes, from the wild words that had no meaning. She felt cold and frightened and wished that she had never ridden abroad this day, that she had never come to the White Roe, that she had never looked upon a thing so terrible in the eyes of one so young. "Candace," she whispered. "What could a woman do to a man to make him feel like that? How much must a man have loved a woman to make him loathe her so?"

She gathered up her wet garments, flung her coat over her shoulder and went out onto the porch. She was standing there, careless of the boisterous wind and the driving rain, when Marc Duclos joined her.

"He will be all right. A few ribs fractured, nothing else I think. With a little quiet his body will be well."

Armande shrugged. "It is of no importance—'Naught broken save this body; lost but breath—'"

Marc said, "I cannot minister to a mind diseased, dear Armande. No one can, the great Shakespeare has

FOG OVER FUNDY

said. One were a fool to try. There is hell in that man's heart."

Armande shivered. "Let us go — quickly."

They got into the car. Before they reached St. Bruno a wan moon staggered out from the rifted, scurrying clouds and glared down on a drowned world. Under that moon Armande rode back to the great house of de Vysart where no light burned to welcome her. She sang *Clair de lune* to raise her own drooping spirits and those of Feu Follet, but the song gay on her lips was mute within her breast. "It is the night, Feu Follet," she said. "We are weary, you and I. Tomorrow the sun will shine. Tomorrow we will be gay."

CHAPTER II

BEAUSEJOUR

OCTOBER sunlight streamed into the room where Armande slept, a white arm flung across her eyes, hair soft as silk a tangled mass on the pillow. In its meshes the gay sunbeams glided and were snarled and held there in that fair prison. A vagrant sun-ray caressed her cheek and slyly darted under the shielding arm and touched the long dark lashes and awakened her.

She loved the moment of awaking. With her it meant greeting the world again, finding its beauties freshened, finding still once more the newness of rapture that perhaps might have faded in the dark of the night preceding. The memory of last night, rushing back to her now, was still unpleasant, though the world, as she had promised Feu Follet, was filled with the glory of the sun.

FOG OVER FUNDY

At her window the thinning vines of the creepers wore spangles of blood-red leaves and clusters of little blue-black berries; far off she could see the uplands of the Tantramar dotted with white farmsteads and striped by wide white roads leading into realms of mystery. Above those distant hills was the deep blue sky across which hurried still the white, broken legions of the storm. The breeze that rustled the vine leaves and swayed the blue-flowered window curtains had in its fresh coolness the little newly cut teeth of the winter being born to the earth. A zesty wind — a wind she loved, speaking of ice-scummed lakes in the heart of the fading forest, of great fires in stone hearths, of the smooth, dark barrels of guns, of the lordly moose and the lonely mallard, and maples red as flame.

She took a cigarette from the black lacquer box on the bedside table, lighted it and watched the blue smoke and thought, there in the warmth of the bed, of last night, of the tempest, the awfulness of the wind, of Damase Blais, the ghostly dikemaster, who somehow didn't seem so terrible this morning; of the White Roe, of the man named John Gower, who had hell in his

BEAUSEJOUR

eyes; who, washed up by the Fundy tides, spoke from the darkness to the girl Candace —

Armande got up, donned a yellow peignoir over black and gold pyjamas, wriggled her feet into snakeskin mules and walked over to the window. Her room was on the topmost floor, the third, in one of the circular towers which, in Norman fashion, made the four corners of the house. As she pushed wide the leaded casements and rested her elbows on the wide sill, the loose sleeves fell away from arms white and rounded, the long gleaming hair showered over her shoulders and she might have been, there in her tower window, some fair lady of the centuries long gone — a Lady of Shallot —

> " And the reapers, reaping early,
> In among the bearded barley,
> Heard a song that echoed clearly —
> 'Tis the Lady of Shallot . . ."

But no reapers worked in the broad fields of the de Vysarts now. The *grands seigneurs,* her forefathers, who looked upon the land and its crops with a warm love, who tended with their own hands the beasts and

FOG OVER FUNDY

the vineyards and the orchards, who ate no food not of their own raising, were gone now and their spirit fled. Only Ulric, the eldest of her family, lived with her at Beausejour; and there was one other brother, Leon, red-headed and wild as a hare, whom they heard from every few years, from South America or China or any other place where there was a war. He had gone to the World War at seventeen, this young de Vysart, and the trade of arms was the only one he knew. Sometimes Armande went to his room and gazed at his flying-helmets, his tunics with the insignia of the Royal Air Force, and thought, with a little catch in her heart, of the tall, freckled lad who used to ride her on his shoulders and tumble her in the grass. That boy, she knew, was forever gone beyond recalling; she had known he was dead the day Leon returned from the war and she had seen a hard man with steel-blue eyes, with a hard deep-lined mouth and the mien of an eagle fretted with the earth. Still she loved him.

Armande looked at the flying clouds and thought of Leon, of whom last they had heard from China, where he was flying planes against the Japs. She looked down

BEAUSEJOUR

at the avenue leading up the hill to the house, between rows of sentinel cedars. Two riders were cantering up the drive. One, she saw, was Ulric, a huge man, red of face and wearing a shock of blond hair like a crest; the other was slighter, with a certain grace remarkable even at that distance. They looked up as she watched them, and waved gaily. Armande waved in answer. She left the window and dressed quickly. It was like Roger Lavergne to arrive at any time, unheralded. He must have come yesterday shortly after she left. She wondered if he and Ulric had slept or if they had sat drinking until dawn and taken the ride to cool off.

She came downstairs, cool in a red sweater and fawn tweed skirt, shod with neat brown brogues, her hair braided across the top of her head. Ulric and Roger Lavergne were in the dining room, eating cold ham and pickles and drinking coffee. They stood up respectfully. Roger came to her, surveying her with frank admiration in his black eyes. He was olive skinned, only slightly taller than Armande. Everything about him, the small-cheque riding-coat, the Bedford cords, the boots of fine soft leather, the snowy linen, bespoke an exquisite-

FOG OVER FUNDY

ness almost feminine; but no woman would ever for a moment think of a feminine streak in him and any man who might would surely learn otherwise to his sorrow.

He bowed low over her hand, touched it lightly with his lips. He smiled at her as he straightened. "Each time I see you, lovely de Vysart, I say there can be no more beauty in the world, then I come again and there are new lights in your hair, new wonders in your eyes."

"And new flatteries upon your lips, m'sieur. And do you make it a point to drop in upon us from the clouds in order to take me by surprise and see if I am always so fair?"

Roger looked at her reproachfully. "I telephoned to Beausejour yesterday from Dorchester. I came by car. Ulric told me you had gone out. I said I knew: there was a wild storm brewing and I know how you love storms. *Mon Dieu,* I am a thoughtless fellow! Here I stand talking and you want breakfast. What shall it be — ham, *brioches,* coffee or ambrosia?"

"I dare say you and Ulric have had enough ambrosia so I'll join you in the coffee and *brioches* and, who

BEAUSEJOUR

knows, maybe a slice of Fidèle's excellent ham. You have been well, Roger, since I saw you at Cap Rouge in August?"

"Well, *ma chère*. You I do not need to ask. And Ulric is not what one would call in failing health."

Ulric looked up from his second plate of ham. He was puffy under the eyes, which were a bit glazed too. "Roger is to be knighted, one hears, in the New Year's honors-list."

"Splendid!" Armande sipped the coffee Roger handed her. "I did not know he was a pork-packer."

Roger laughed gaily. "Right, Armande. And not being one, I should have been raised to the peerage. No doubt when I print a few good scandals in the papers my father built and bequeathed me, I shall be made a lord. Merit — merit, my dear friends." He looked severely at Armande. "Give an account of yourself, woman of the night. I heard you pussy-footing upstairs at cock-light. It is a miracle the de Vysarts don't fall from their frames and crush the degenerate daughter of their house. Where were you?"

"I don't know." Armande frowned. There came an

absent look into her eyes. She started, feeling their curious glances. "I mean, of course, that one can be in very definite and concrete places and still not know where one was. Now was I in a nightmare or a— *Ecoutez!* I was only a short way from *le grand carrefour* — the cross-roads — at Pré des Capucins when the storm broke. So I went to Isaac Proux's Inn — you have been there, Roger — the White Roe, thinking I would stay there.

"At the height of the storm, as the old men around the fire spoke of Damase Blais, the drowned dikemaster — one of our local legends — a white face appeared at the inn-window and we found a man on the porch, a man who had been cast up by the sea. I went to St. Bruno and brought Marc Duclos to look after him—"

"You rode through that storm!" Roger set down his cup and stared at her.

"It was nothing. The man might have died. Marc fixed him." She could not bring herself to tell them of what, more than the pain of his broken body, had ailed that man; she could not speak of Candace or of how

BEAUSEJOUR

Marc Duclos had said he could not "minister to a mind diseased." She wondered why she could not tell big Ulric and Roger Lavergne the whole story. Perhaps because, in the light of this morning, when the rain-washed, storm-purged earth was so stark and real, those things that had happened seemed merely figments of an imagination disordered and unstrung.

"Who was this man? Where did he come from?" demanded Ulric, breaking a *brioche* with a great crackling of crisp crust.

Armande nibbled at a pickle. "His name was John Gower. He was a sailor on the Yacht Triton. Wrecked, I imagine. Probably he was the only one who escaped."

"Fools!" growled Ulric. "They should build a wall across the mouth of the Bay of Fundy, have one gate in it and keep all yachtsmen out. They would litter our shore with wreckage and corpses if God were not so good to imbeciles."

"It was an interesting experience, Armande," said Roger. "But then, things are always happening in this land of Cocagne and Tantramar. The fishermen catch mermaids and golden minnows in their nets, the plough-

FOG OVER FUNDY

shares are ever turning up cannon-balls or rusty sabres, the women are witches and weave patterns of men's lives on their looms."

"It is a lovely land, Roger."

"Better than Quebec? Better than Mo'real? Ah, there is a city."

"Not for me." Armande shook her bright head. "Here I have my roots and my being. Keep your Japanese gardens at the Ritz, your promenades on Dufferin Terrace and your skijoring at Lucerne — give me the dikes and the marshes and the sea and the wild geese winging north."

"Maid of the Misty Marshlands," laughed Roger. "To me it gives a feeling of loneliness, of terrible solitude. So many monotonous, unrelieved miles of meadows, and the net-reels in the fishing villages, like gibbets, and your dark and dour peasants with their sullen Norman stinginess — "

"They are not stingy," Armande's cheeks reddened.

Roger's teeth flashed white. He bowed humbly. "Frugality then — with their lovable Norman frugality

BEAUSEJOUR

that would squeeze a cent until the king's image has lockjaw."

"You are only trying to bring on an argument, Roger." Armande finished her coffee and stood up. "This morning I do not feel like arguing. Even talk — even such brilliant talk as must, of necessity, for one acts according to one's nature, and Buffon has well said — ' the style is the man himself — ' where was I? — oh, yes — must come from the brilliant proprietor-editor of Quebec's oldest and most illustrious journals — what are their names? — even such gems of wit and culture seem as nothing compared with the fact that the sea will gleam like silver today and that perhaps tomorrow the moose will be covered with frost when they burst out of the forests and plunge into the lakes."

"Ah, that does sound good. One never forgets that sight, of a frosty morning, when the hand shivers that holds the gun, when the great moose looks like a ghost, all rimed with glistening frost in the gray light of dawn. I do not blame you for not listening to me now. Presently — " His eyes compelled her, and his voice, so low and soft — " Presently, though, I may speak of other things that are not so light on the lip. We shall join you later, *mignonne*."

Armande went out into the brightness of the morning. Autumn had touched the land; the green of the marshes, despite the abundant rain, was turning to a paler hue, soon it would become yellow, then dun; the spears of the willows and the little coin-shaped poplar leaves were faded and showering down upon the lawns of Beausejour; the maples, gay harlequins, flaunted their carnival garb of varied golds and scarlets and the chattering squirrels darted madly about the beeches. From the farm buildings on the slope behind the house the intermittent singing whine of a rotary saw cut through the air and a motor chug-chugged ceaselessly as great logs of rock-maple and beech were cut against the coming of winter. Across the dike-ribbed flat of the marshes the river squirmed like a silver anaconda and poured its flood into the glinting waters of the bay.

These were the sights and sounds that Armande loved; the blue smoke rising from low stone chimneys, the bark of vigilant collies, the lowing of the Holsteins, the Herefords and Polled-Angus that grazed upon the

BEAUSEJOUR

upland meadows, and the slow mellow tinkle of their bells. Sirdar, a huge white Afghan hound that Leon had sent to her four years ago, came loping from the kennels behind the house and climbed the broad steps to nuzzle her hand and press his great bulk against her.

Presently, Roger came out and stood beside her, hands in pockets, smoking an Egyptian cigarette that desecrated the freshness of the morning. He stood in silence for a while, and she was glad. There are so many hateful, banal things that one can say at the start of the morning — things that will jar and rankle all the day through until the twilight comes, bringing peace and rest.

"Ulric," he said at length, " will go to his study to go over some work pertaining to the farm. He is always in the middle of it; never gets any further."

"Never any further," agreed Armande.

" He was not made for the land."

"The land is made for us, dear Roger, and simple toil, to make free of the quotation, is a great deal more than Norman blood. De Vysarts have been soldiers or tillers of the soil: Ulric is not a soldier like Leon."

FOG OVER FUNDY

"*Soit*. Let it go. You have not heard from Leon of late?"

"Not since more than six months ago. He was then in China."

"He is now in New York. I saw him there briefly one afternoon a month ago at the St. Moritz."

"But — I do not understand — he returned home, to America, and did not let us know! It is not like Leon."

"He was never the one to write, Armande. You know that."

"But you talked with him? He was well? He spoke of us?"

"But yes. Of course he spoke of you — mostly of you. He asked for Ulric, for Beausejour, for St. Bruno, for people I had never heard of — the mayor, the curé, the notary, the school-teacher. He seemed hungry for news of home."

Armande shook her head. She looked full in Roger's eyes. "More. There is more. Tell me."

"No more. I assure you I saw him for only a few moments."

"He was alone?"

BEAUSEJOUR

"Little Inquisitor! Fair Torquemada! He was not alone: he was with a woman."

"And — ?"

"A very lovely woman."

"Of course. Ah well, long ago I gave up worrying about Leon."

"I know. That is why I told you. I thought you and Ulric knew he was home, but when I mentioned it to Ulric yesterday, he was quite as amazed as you. No doubt Leon will be dropping in one of these days. He was ever the one for the bizarre and unexpected."

"I hope he comes soon, Roger."

"You love him very much?"

"He was always a bit of a god to me — so strong, so brave and gallant. He was lost in this world of ours. He was a gentleman of France." It came to her with a piercing sudden shock that she spoke in the past tense. She clutched Roger's arm. He stared at her, concerned. He laid his hand over hers. "Come. That wild heart of yours, that spirit ruled more by instinct, by senses far beyond the five we ordinary mortals have, will yet do you harm. Let us get my car and go for a drive."

FOG OVER FUNDY

" Yes. Yes, I should like that."

" Good! You get a coat. I shall have the car around by the time you return."

Ulric was still in the dining room. He had finished pouring himself a generous drink. He lifted it to his lips with hand that shook. Armande, passing the door, frowned darkly. She would be glad when Leon came. She would try to make Leon stay at home. He, with his brilliance, his restless energy, could again make something of the fine estate that Ulric was letting go to seed. Give Ulric tobacco and liquor and horses and he required nothing further. But in his love of all these he was a spendthrift and knew no satiation of his appetite. Women, fortunately, he bothered with very little. His wife had been killed in a motor-smash on their honeymoon. Armande had never known him to grieve very much.

When, with a gray polo-coat on her arm, she returned to the piazza, Roger's car, a black and silver Daimler, its Quebec number-plates still caked with good Acadian mud, was waiting there. He moved over for her. " Drive. My nerves are quite steady. I fully recovered a week

BEAUSEJOUR

ago from the time you took me to Three Rivers last August. This time I shall shut my eyes."

"This time I shall not drive fast. If you lived a good life, Roger, you would not worry about my driving."

"To think that such old wisdom should dwell on lips so young! *Ma foi!* But I do lead a good life — a splendid life, though a lonely one — and that is why I do not care to die. There is so much to live for, Armande."

"You do love life very much, Roger."

"So much, child, that it hurts."

"I too find it like that. Fold down the windscreen. Let us feel the sea-wind on our faces." She slowed the car and Roger unscrewed the gadgets and folded down the glass. The wind rippled past their ears. It was like riding through some ethereal water, so cool, so refreshing. The great motor pulsed softly, the huge tires whined on the drying clay and cackled raucously on the mile of paving that led into St. Bruno and was the village-pride.

"I love this, Roger."

"I love you, Armande."

She did not answer. She felt those warm dark eyes

FOG OVER FUNDY

upon her. She felt a heat in her cheeks that the wind could not cool. She saw her knuckles whiten as her hands clutched the wheel. He loved her. He had had the right to tell her so this ten years past, for it was agreed of old by their families that she should be his. He was a man, Roger; he had never before spoken to her of love and it was like him to speak now thus casually of it on a morning drive.

"You are not angry, Ma'm'selle de Vysart?"

"But no, M'sieur Lavergne. I am — am proud and honored and humble."

"No, Armande — none of those things. I should not have spoken perhaps. You are not ready yet to listen."

"I — that I do not know."

"I shall wait then for a moon and I shall hire a most seductive string orchestra to play the Barcarolle from Contes de Hoffman. I shall have a gondola imported from Hollywood and ride with you down the Bay of Fundy — and bon-bons — I shall buy you a huge box of bon-bons. All girls love them."

"You talk lightly, Roger. I wonder if the rest of the

BEAUSEJOUR

world sees as clearly through the jester's masque as I do."

He caught her wrist in fingers of steel. "Don't say that!" The soft gentle voice had become harsh. "The jester's masque! What put it into that young head of yours that I should wear a masque?"

"I know it from the senses beyond the ordinary five—those special senses with which you have endowed me. You laugh, you are gay, you are beloved, you are wealthy, you are brilliant, but—"

"Spare me, Armande!" He was laughing now. "Witch of the Tantramar, you can see into a man's soul. I will hear no more from you. If I listened I should probably hear all about myself and thus I should make my own acquaintance—something which, for many years, I have studiously avoided. Please, Armande, tell me no more. Do not even tell me that you love me; merely that you love no one else."

"I love no one else."

"Drive on. I die content. Hello!" He sat up. "The entire population of St. Bruno, the whole three hundred and fifty souls, dogs, goats and the like not counted,

FOG OVER FUNDY

seems to be gathered in the market place—"

The Daimler slid to a stop on the outskirts of the crowd. "*Holà*, Paul Emil!" Armande called to a big-eyed little boy with tawny curls, who sported sea boots so large that one of them could easily have accommodated both his feet. "What is going on here?"

The little boy came shyly to the car and stood upon the running board. His blue eyes then were on a level with Armande's. She flung an arm about his neck. Roger watched them with a smile. Momentarily it faded and his thick brows drew down. He was smiling once more when the boy looked from Armande to him. "It is the wreck, ma'm'selle. It is a great horror, M'sieur. One, two, t'ree body they have find. It was a yacht, one says, of the rich Americans. Of it there is nothing left. At mass this morning, Père Archambault pray for the repose of their souls. One says that at *le grand carrefour*, at the White Roe Inn, is a man, the only one who has escape this wreck."

Armande nodded. "Thank you, Paul Emil." She smiled into the boy's eyes. Roger watched her curiously and looked, then, off across the dimpling waters beyond

BEAUSEJOUR

the tumbledown wharves of St. Bruno. Fishing-boats showed their white wings out there and cruisers poked around inshore. "Bits of matchwood and bodies shrouded with sea-weed," muttered Roger.

Léandre Frechette, the local poet and romancer, came to the car to announce for the benefit of M'sieur Lavergne that he, the humble but earnest correspondent of those great papers M'sieur Lavergne owned, had wired complete details — or as complete as one could expect — to Quebec.

"Even," said Léandre who had a thin nose, horse-teeth, a huge Adam's apple and a Lloyd George haircut, "I went to the White Roe Inn to interview the seaman who escaped and found shelter there. But he would not talk, beyond saying that he remembered nothing. His name we know — John Gower. The owner of the yacht was M'sieur Loring, of New York. At the office they can check up on all details."

"You have done well, my friend." Roger patted the shoulder of this astute journalist whose biggest scoop to this date had been the story of a man from Michigan mistaking an ancient mare of Dominique Le Blanc's

FOG OVER FUNDY

for the famous white deer of Tantramar and laying the poor creature low. "Your fame is assured, my good Frechette. Mademoiselle de Vysart and I shall drive on now to the White Roe to have a look at this survivor. *Au-revoir.*"

"I did not tell him of the part you played, Armande. A newspaper man would make a story of it that would combine all the heroic qualities of the man who brought the news from Ghent to Aix, Paul Revere and Laura Secord."

"Thanks for keeping quiet then."

"Not at all," grinned Roger. "I shall write it up myself and send it in."

"I shall sue you for libel."

"That is the main function of newspaper-proprietors. Our slogan is 'No day without its lawsuit. Sue away!'"

They rolled along the road below the dike. The marsh-clay, even after the awful deluge, was drying fast, but great puddles still lingered and sent showers of mud and water spattering against the fenders. At different places crews of men were at work repairing the

BEAUSEJOUR

dikes where the furious onslaught of the sea had torn and broken them.

"This road last night," said Roger musingly, "must have seemed like hell's Main Street. Armande, I do not know how you do the things you do. Were you not timid? Were you not—? *Sapree!* I talk like a fool. You were never timid or afraid of anything. But it was a tremendous thing to do for a stranger, for anyone."

"I did not mind it much. Right here, where the tree has fallen partly across the road, the water came to Feu Follet's saddle-girths and shortly after we passed the tree she all but threw me into the mud. After that we had little trouble."

They drove into the yard at the White Roe, over the cobbles washed clean and fresh by the rain. Even the windows shone and the noble albino deer on the signboard that projected from the porch was so scoured that her ribs had almost vanished. The geraniums of Elodie's careful tending showed their pretty red blooms in the windows, and the air as they entered was lush with the goodly odor of frying shad.

Isaac, in a fresh white apron—he looked for a con-

FOG OVER FUNDY

siderable rush of business today and much free advertising when the newspaper men arrived from Monckton — polished tumblers behind the well-lined bar. He hurried out to greet them, with many obeisances, many solicitously expressed hopes that Ma'm'selle de Vysart had suffered no ill consequences from her so heroic conduct. "It was, M'sieur Lavergne, a deed which, I feel sure, though I am a poor man and have neither travelled much nor read, is quite unrivalled in the history of our people."

"Beginning next term it shall be taught to the young ones in the schools," Roger assured him gravely. "It was a splendid thing and I know it was worthwhile. It perhaps meant this man's life. He is better now? He is much improved?"

"Much, m'sieur. The Doctor Duclos came again from St. Bruno early this morning to see him. He will rest here for a while until his ribs have renewed themselves; then he will be well again."

"One is permitted to see him?" asked Armande.

"But of course —" Isaac led the way upstairs to the brighter room whither they had moved this so im-

BEAUSEJOUR

portant and profitable guest who had already attracted much welcome trade. "He is a very stern young man, this M'sieur Gow-er, and I fear — " Isaac stopped on the landing, turned around, tapped his temple with a forefinger and winked with ineffable slyness. "He said if I let anyone else into his room he would throw them out the window. That, of course, does not apply to Ma'm'selle Armande, who saved his life and to whom he will be forever in debt — "

He knocked as he spoke upon the door of the room at the stair-head where Armande had eaten supper last night. He pushed open the door and they followed him in. It was lovely there today and cheerful with gay crisp curtains, flowers and bright pictures.

"Get out!" said a voice from the bed, a voice still weak yet very determined. "I told you to bring no one in here — no one. Can't you understand! Hang it all — am I to be made a poppy-show for every rustic sight-seer. You Shylock you! I do believe you are charging two-bits to let them in to have a peek at me. Please go, you people, I — I am very tired — "

"I am very sorry — " Armande stepped forward and

looked into his face, into a pair of wide-set brown eyes in which this morning there was still the lurking ghost, a demoniac ghost, of what last night she had seen there.

"I don't want to seem ungracious," he said, frowning, "but I do not think I know you. I have seen you somewhere — "

"Yes," cut in Roger suavely, "you have. She saved your life by riding through a strip of hell last night. Perhaps you'd like to thank her or are you too tired for that?"

The pale cheeks flushed. He looked away from Armande, from Roger's mocking eyes. "I am sorry — I am very sorry I was so — so rude. I know something of what you did — not all. But with my whole heart I thank you, Miss — "

"de Vysart."

"de Vysart!" He jerked on the bed in his effort to sit up. His face was contorted.

"Ah, *mon Dieu!*" Armande came and knelt by him. "We excite you. You are still in pain."

He stared into her eyes for a moment. His own closed then and his hand covered them, shut out from her gaze

BEAUSEJOUR

the sight of that look of the pit that had come there again.

"I am — still in pain," he muttered, and said no more and made no move; so Armande, very silent, and Roger, very puzzled, and Isaac, very abashed, tiptoed from the room.

CHAPTER III

LITANY

ARMANDE and Roger drove on up the coast to a place called the Devil's Cauldron, where the in-rushing tide swirled and boiled and bubbled like a maelstrom in a huge rocky pit. From the rim, sixty some feet above the hurly-burly of foaming water, they gazed down upon it.

"'Double, double, toil and trouble; fire burn and cauldron bubble,'" said Roger. "I don't know what to make of your mysterious man of the sea, Armande. At first, he seemed a surly enough sort of fellow; at the end he was rather pathetic."

"Yes." Armande plucked a straw and broke it in four pieces, then broke each bit into two more. "I dare say it is all due to the shock. He will recover soon and go his way."

LITANY

"He did not talk as one would expect an ordinary seaman to talk. But then, one can never tell in these days from what a man does whether he is a Ph.D. or a peasant. Then, too, there are excellent mail-order courses which in five lessons will guarantee to teach a dumb man how to make spell-binding after-dinner speeches. Handsome chap, this John Gower."

"Yes." Armande frowned. "He intrigues me. At the same time I do not relish being treated as a busybody when I come to ask about his health."

"I fancy he will not treat you so again."

"There will be no again."

"Why should there be?" Roger flung his cigarette-end into the Devil's Cauldron and watched it vanish. He looked up at the sky. He looked into Armande's eyes. "They are still more blue," he said, "and your skin is gold and rose and ivory. Armande, I am rash, I know; I tempt Destiny. But I have waited long and something tells me if I wait longer, it will be too late. I love you, Armande, with all the love that this poor heart is capable of. You were right about me — about my wearing the jester's masque, the cap-and-bells and rattling dried peas in a pig's bladder. A man of the world—" He laughed. "At heart I feel afraid sometimes—and hideously alone. Come with me, stay with me always. Let me find sanctuary in your love, let me hide my face against your breast."

He bent to her, his eyes earnest, pleading, almost piteous in their pleading. Roger Lavergne—soon to be a knight; a great man, a wealthy man, beloved of the multitude, with the finest fruits of life his for the plucking. Only a boy's eyes looked into hers and a boy's heart cried out to her. She laid her cool palms against his cheeks and gazed into his eyes for a moment. She drew his head against her young breast and smoothed his thick black hair and kissed it.

"Is—is it my answer, Armande?" She felt his body tremble.

"What more then?" she whispered. "You are so good, so fine."

"It is nothing. I am not. You—do love me, Armande? You said you loved no other man; but do you love me?"

"I—I do not know. There is something warm in my

LITANY

breast and I love to hold you so."

"But—" With sudden, terrifying strength he caught her to him and possessed her lips. He felt her body stiffen, felt the pressure of her hands against his shoulders, saw outrage and horror in her eyes. Trembling, he released her; put her away from him, and stood up. His shoulders seemed to droop, a lock of his hair encroached upon the olive skin of his brow. Impatiently he brushed it back. He did not look at her.

"A priestess," he said, " is outraged before the High Altar and the wrath of that god she serves shall smite him who thus profanes the holy of holies. I am sorry, Armande— more sorry than I can tell you. But I have my answer."

"No." She bit her trembling lip, tried to still the tremors of her body that felt hot and harmed. "That could give you no answer. I—"

"No other man has ever held you like that, kissed you like that —"

"No other."

"You hated it."

FOG OVER FUNDY

"From you, it did not seem — well, it did not seem like you, Roger."

"Oh, God!" She heard his teeth click. "What am I anyway? A monk, a saint — ? I am a man, Armande; with all a man's needs and hungers. And you, *mignonne*, are human, and very warm and very sweet. You must have a woman's hunger for love. If I do not stimulate that hunger nor offer it any satisfaction, then I am not for you. It may be that your appetite craves caviar and I am only black pudding. Forgive me, I merely talk. Perhaps I should take you, force you, make you love me, awaken in that lovely body of yours what some other man must some day awaken."

"And then you would hate me."

"Hate you." He looked sharply at her, his eyes clouded, his mouth bitter and sullen. "Remembering this day perhaps I should hate you: most surely I will hate him."

"But there is no other."

"You are sure? What about Marc Duclos, that strong, earnest young doctor, once a peasant's brat, in whose life you have ever shone as a pure star, who

LITANY

gazed into your dear eyes as he dissected frogs and dreamed of you as he carved out people's appendixes! Who chucked up a great chance in Paris and a better one in Montreal to bury himself in a lot of marsh mud just so he could be near you — what of him?"

"You are cruel, Roger. You who are so fine are being too unkind. You are not yourself —"

"For once I am myself, minus the fool's masque. Perhaps I shall never wear it again, Armande; certainly before you I can never wear it with any hope of fooling you. So there is nothing about Duclos?"

"Only that he is a man." She stood up, dusting her skirt. Her cheeks were crimson and there was a dangerous light in her eyes. "Only that, with much more grace than you, light of the salons and grace of the boulevards and soon to be Knight Commander of the Order of St. Michael and St. George — only that this 'once a peasant's brat' took his disappointment much more like a man and never spoke of the hungers of his flesh."

Lavergne shrugged. He bowed in token of defeat. "*Touché!*" he said quietly. "The great lady speaks now and I feel that somewhere in the Lavergnes the

FOG OVER FUNDY

mongrel strain crept in. Need I say that I am sorry?"

"You need say nothing, Roger." She laid her hand on his sleeve. "It is I who should be ashamed and abashed — and I am. Let us go now."

They turned away from the rumbling and hissing of the Cauldron and walked through the fields to the car. All that could be said had been said. There was nothing more. She left the wheel to Roger and, though all the way back to Beausejour he drove as one whom the fiends pursue, she did not once protest. She thought, and with reason, at times, as the car dashed through covered bridges that shook and protested, as it skidded on still wet clay, that he had it in his mind to kill them both; but she said nothing. When the car grated to a stop in the gravel of Beausejour, he leaned over and patted her hand. "I shall say goodby now in case I do not see you again before I go. I find I must hurry back to Montreal. I shall take time only to gather up my things. Do not think too hard of me, Armande. After all, I loved you."

"I know." She turned away, her mouth uneasy, her eyes misted. "I know, Roger, I am sorry. I shall be

LITANY

sorrier when you go — perhaps I shall be always sorry."

"No! No, I think not." He smiled, looking at his hands. "At eighteen love is a tremendously serious business; at thirty-five it is, I hear, tempered a bit by philosophy. And I am thirty-five, *chère* — but I was never much of a philosopher. Adieu, Armande. Go quickly. Stand for a moment on the topmost step and turn and look at me so that always I may remember you so."

She flung her arms about his neck and kissed him and looked into his eyes. " Remember me like this, Roger — always."

She left him then, hurried up the steps and into the house. In the drawing-room off the hall Marc Duclos was standing. She saw bitterness in his eyes. She knew its source. He had come to the window when he heard the car. He had seen. Well, if he chose to think like that, let him. She could not explain now. It was all she could do to talk. Her heart-beats were running wild and her mind raced, raced and would not be still.

"I was passing." Marc did not look at her. He could

FOG OVER FUNDY

not. "I came to tell you that the man John Gower is much improved. But perhaps you knew—"

"I was there, to the White Roe, this morning. Roger went with me. We saw John Gower. He was not very pleasant to me."

"He is unnerved of course. It will take time. There were six, he told me, on the yacht. All of the others perished. He is a strange man. He said, 'It would be my luck to get through.'"

"You mean—he wanted to die!"

"It would seem so."

"But he is so young."

"I too am young," said Marc. "You will forgive me, Armande, I must go." He walked to the door. "I too could have wealth and a title and—" His face was contorted. He hurried away. He passed Roger in the hall and did not see him. Armande watched him stride down the drive, liking the strength in his thick, rather short figure, the energy of his walk. "This seems to be my day for losing my best friends. It has been an ugly day. All the men I have met have growled at me or glowered at me or wept over me. There is only Ulric

LITANY

left to quarrel with — unless Leon arrives — "

She went to her room and bathed. She felt weary in her soul today and the memory of Roger's embrace still left her hot and uneasy. Strange; but not until the moment of that abandoned caress had she really known she did not love Roger. Not until his mouth moved and burned against her crushed lips had she realized what love could be — how wondrous or how ugly.

"But is that love — to desire my body so, to burn for it, to want to destroy it!" She closed her eyes, shook her head as if to drive away some evil vision; her lips moved. "I saw it in his eyes and I hated it and he, at that moment, hated me for having seen so deep within him. Are all men like that — underneath? Marc Duclos, is he like that, seeking of me only what Roger seeks? That, I feel, is not love. Love would be a stronger thing without passion," she finished with young wisdom as a knock sounded sharply on the panels of her door.

"Come, please."

The door opened. Ulric rolled in, huge, his face brick-red, his blonde hair so upended that one could not guess how it had thinned on the top. He came to her and

FOG OVER FUNDY

stood, great legs a-straddle in front of her. His watch-charm, a little gold lanthorn swinging on a great gold chain, was on a level with her eyes. It had been her father's. She thought of that now, of how she used to tug at it, barely able to reach so high. Ulric, she noticed, was getting terribly paunchy. She loathed men with stomachs.

" Roger has gone," rumbled Ulric. " Why were you not there to see him off? It is only the part of hospitality to speed the parting guest, and if people like us do not observe such points of etiquette we are no better than peasants."

"But observing them will make us better than peasants? "

" Eh? Yes, yes, of course." Ulric was always a little non-plussed by her. " Why not? "

" Well then, why so? Don't be medieval, Ulric. If you want to be truly medieval, read up on the lives of your fore-fathers and model your conduct accordingly. You like central-heating and electrics and motors and all the things of today — except today's ideas. Peasants, you say — there are no peasants any more: they have

LITANY

all become dictators and commissars and whatnot."

"You chatter so. You put me off. Why did you not come down to say goodby to Roger?"

"Because I said goodby before I came up."

"You two did not quarrel?"

"Not what you'd call a quarrel really. Perhaps a mild disagreement."

"Confound it, don't quibble!" Ulric's cheeks looked like hot stove lids now and the pupils of his glassy blue eyes were dilated. "You know you're going to marry Roger, don't you? Did he speak of marriage?"

"He did. I gather that's what he was driving at. I told him I didn't love him."

"Didn't — didn't what!"

"You wouldn't understand, Ulric. You will understand this: I am never going to marry Roger Lavergne."

"You fool!" Ulric's big fists clenched and he raised and lowered them. "You little fool! Why did you say a thing like that? Suppose he should take you at your word. Suppose he should believe you and never return here!"

FOG OVER FUNDY

"That is probably what he will do. It means nothing to me."

"But — but this marriage — " Ulric rubbed his head with his knuckles. He had believed in this marriage as earnestly as he believed that the moon affected the weather — "it was all arranged by our parents. You and — "

"I was not consulted," said Armande.

"Consulted! You were only seven or eight years old!"

"Age of Reason, just the same. Anyway, why all the fuss? What's it to you?"

"I — I — why it means — why, I had my heart set on it. I never thought of anything different. You don't know what you're doing, Armande — " he pleaded clumsily — " Roger will soon be a knight. You will be Lady Lavergne — "

"As far as that goes, my brother, I am Armande de Vysart, and one of my forebears was the Comtesse de Valois and, were I title-minded, which I'm not, I shouldn't worry about a pork-baron's or a brewer's order of dubious merit."

LITANY

"That — that is terrible, Armande! I think you are becoming mad. You will get over this. I will write to Roger and tell him that it is just a young girl's nonsense. That's all it is, isn't it?"

"No!" She stood up, facing him and her eyes, clear and angry, never faltered from his. "It is not nonsense. It is the truth. I don't love Roger. I shall never marry him —"

"We won't discuss it further, you — you witch! You vixen! You are a disgrace to the name you bear —"

"That I am not, Ulric." Her mouth quivered, then hardened. "That I am not and could never be. Do not plague me now. Do not, I tell you!" Her own fists were clenched and she took a step towards Ulric and comically before her willowy advance he gave back — he so large, like an elephant before a gazelle.

"Very well," he said. "But it is not ended."

"It is ended." She turned her back on him, spoke over her shoulder. "What of Leon? He told you he had seen Leon in New York — with a woman?"

"Yes, he told me that. What of it? What am I to do? I cannot keep track of Leon."

FOG OVER FUNDY

"Has he spent all his money? I mean all save what was left with you in trust?"

"Yes. Well, I guess so. I — I tell you I know nothing of him. He is wild, a scatter-brain like you. The only thing in his favor is that he does not stay at home here to plague me."

"When he comes home he will stay," said Armande softly. "He comes home to stay."

"How can you know that? Did Roger — ?"

"Roger told me nothing. I think he knew nothing. But I know I can keep Leon at home. I can show him that he is needed here. He must stay, for his sake, if not for yours and mine."

"Mine — what is it to me if he stays?" Ulric blustered.

"You have let things go. You know it —"

"See here, I will not have a brat of a girl talk to me this way. I have given you too much rein —"

"You have never held rein on me. You forget I have my own money — at least, I will have it in a few years. It is only in your care, you know. But you have failed badly, Ulric, as head of the house of de Vysart. You

LITANY

have done well with horses and dogs and you are, I know, a supreme authority on cognac and on how a ragout should be made. Apart from that—"

"You are insolent; you are brazen. You shall marry Lavergne just as soon as he wants you. Mind that, milady!"

"You cannot force me. No one can. You've lived too long away from the world, Ulric. Girls don't marry like that now-a-days. We wait for love to come along; when it does, we take it, no matter if the man be prince or peasant. Leon, when he comes, will be on my side, should I need him."

"I hope then," snarled Ulric, "that he never comes. Why should you set him above me? What has he ever done except roam around the world and shoot down a lot of poor devils who probably didn't know how to defend themselves!"

"You are wrong," said Armande softly. "Very wrong. Leon was always brave, always the grand gentleman."

"Easy to be, *in absentia*." Ulric swung around on his heel and stumbled out of the room. Armande kept her back to him. She could not even imagine the chagrin,

FOG OVER FUNDY

the abject fear that caused the muscles of his face to twitch. The fine network of veins close to the skin of his cheeks looked like some weird maps drawn in crimson; his breath came hard as if a steel hand were closing on his windpipe. She had upset all his world. She did not know just how much her marriage to Roger Lavergne's wealth could mean to Ulric, nor did Roger himself, nor did anyone.

Ulric returned to his room. He tried a thousand times to reassure himself, to make himself believe that this talk with Armande was not real; that within the year she and Roger would be married and all would again be well with him. Let things go — he grinned mirthlessly into his glass when he thought how very little Armande knew of how far he had let things go. But always he had gone on the assumption that soon there would be a close alliance between his family and the Lavergnes, who counted their wealth in millions. If Armande were in earnest — But she could not be! She was young, very young. Girls at her age, he had a vague idea, were a bit crazy, were apt to say one thing and do another. Tomorrow, no doubt, she would be sorry for the way

LITANY

she had acted. When Roger came again she would welcome him and fling herself into his arms.

And Leon — what was all this talk of Leon? Suppose, he, Ulric, had not made a go of looking after their fortunes, why turn now and pin so much faith on a chap like Leon, who was about as stable as a windmill. More of Armande's nonsense. Always, he remembered bitterly, Leon and Armande had allied themselves against him. He was older and he did not mind being excluded from their games and their secrets, but he most certainly would mind if Leon came back home to stay and tried to set himself up as head of the house.

He wouldn't have that. No, by heaven, not for a moment would he have it. "I'll see him and her dead before I'll take a back seat in this house." He banged his glass on the chair arm, and it shattered. He stared at it stupidly and began to cry. He drank from the bottle presently. He fell asleep. His snores were loud in the big, dark-panelled room — an ugly sound that was somehow uglier in the grand cool stillness of the afternoon. From their shadowy places on the wall dead and gone de Vysarts looked down on him as he lay there

FOG OVER FUNDY

sodden and abandoned, sleeping through the long bright hours of too short life.

Armande lingered a while in her room; stood in the same spot by the window, her proud straight back still turned to the door that had slammed on Ulric. Her thoughts were at once bitter and hopeful: bitter against Ulric, against his stupidity, his sottishness, his utter lack of concern for her own happiness; hopeful that in Leon she would find the strength, the understanding and sympathy she so much needed. Her mother had died a year after she was born, her father when she was ten. Leon had been mostly absent. Ulric had made no effort ever to give her companionship or understanding. She had gone to school to the nuns at Sault aux Recollets, in Quebec, and for a while to Havergal, but she had learned more in the long lonely hours of riding over the marshes and into the hills, of lying among the tall daisies and buttercups and watching the white clouds in the blue, of sitting at the organ in the Church of St. Bruno and improvising strange, wild melodies that made the good curé bless himself — than ever she had learned from books.

LITANY

At last, weary of thinking, finding that thoughts of Ulric tangled with thoughts of Roger and these with thoughts of Marc Duclos, she donned her riding togs and left the room. In the kitchen she ate sandwiches and drank milk at the great table the servants used — there was only fat Leonie, the cook, now, and Benoit, Ulric's man, and a useless maid named Claudette. Fidèle Thibodeau kept the home-farm. They laughed secretly at Ulric, the servants, but looked on Armande with a mixture of adoration and fear: so often she seemed to live in another world, so often her eyes seemed to see things that they could not see. She loved all things that most people feared and avoided — the thunder, the mad lightning, the bitter cold of the Acadian winter. They whispered to each other, as did the good habitants of St. Bruno, that she was a re-incarnation of some great lady of long ago, that she had the second sight, perhaps the evil eye.

And in St. Bruno was the little boy, Paul Emil Delagarde, who was her image, that same boy who had stood on the running-board of Roger Lavergne's car and told them about the wreck. Her image, yet he was

FOG OVER FUNDY

most certainly the son of Suzanne Delagarde and of Gregoire, the fisherman, who had been drowned most mysteriously before the child was born. Of all their weird beliefs and imaginings, their rustling whispers as she passed, Armande knew nothing. She liked the little Delagarde, but had never noticed in him the strange likeness to herself that Roger's quick eyes had at once remarked. She loved the people, loved to go into their neat cottages, eat at their homely boards and sing with them and dance. That she moved among them as one apart, as one whom their superstitious hearts could not accept as being of their own clay, never once occurred to her. She had her own thoughts always and lived in a world of her own, peopled with images of beauty, where the sunsets were always fair, the green woods always enchanted, the rivers always flowing smooth and the flowers fadeless. She had been forced into that world by solitude and now it was more real to her than the world she lived in.

She went to the stable with lumps of sugar for Feu Follet — the Will o' the Wisp. The mare greeted her eagerly, nuzzled her shoulder, studied her with great

LITANY

eyes. Again today they would go, free and happy, over the meadows and into cool green forests perhaps and across rippling brooks of clear cold water. "No errands of mercy today, *mon amie*," said Armande as the stableboy saddled the mare and bridled her. "Last night we gave of our best, you and I, and though we sought no gratitude, it is most certain we got none — at least, as far as I could see. However, Mr. John Gower may have strange ways of expressing his thanks. Who cares?"

Who cared, indeed. She thought of John Gower as Feu Follet, stepping high, carried her down the drive and out onto the Post Road, white and dusty now, dried by the heat of the sun. A strange young man, and no doubt a very brave and hardy one. How else had he won his way to shore without being drowned, without being impaled on the rocks or smashed against the seawalls. She thought of that young face, those fine eyes that were made for laughter but held instead the look of the damned. "I shall not see him again. I shall never learn about him, unless Marc should find out and perhaps tell me. But Marc is furious at me because he thinks I love Roger, while Ulric is furious because he

FOG OVER FUNDY

thinks I don't. *Hélas!* What is one to do?"

One could do nothing now but ride along the road to Pre d'en haut between thinning hedges, under the drooping willows that showered their dry leaves softly down. But there was beauty in the Autumn. Armande loved it, of all seasons, best. The trees on the distant hills were like a crazy-quilt, a coat-of-many-colors — lovely, ephemeral scarlets, golds and yellows, with the always constant dark green of the firs and the paler green of spruce and cedar. Far above the Tantramar a flock of wild geese, a smooth, swinging cohort, winged its southward way and distantly she heard their honking cry and did not envy but wondered at them.

At the farms she passed the men had begun to bank their houses high with earth and great piles of hardwood were stacked outside each kitchen-door; on the marsh the big haycocks stood trim and solid and the barns were filled to bursting and the cellars stored well with the fruits of the field and orchard. By many a farmyard gate she stopped to chat with sturdy Jean or stout Marie, to smile at the brown-faced, dark-eyed children, to drink cold water from wells where the bucket hung

LITANY

on a balance-pole after the Acadian fashion.

The sun was dipping down into a deep red sky when she passed the White Roe. She gave it a careless look and wondered for a brief moment why she had gone so many miles by a roundabout way. It was not of course, she told herself impatiently, because of the stranger lying there in the big room at the stair head. Why should it be? She could see the window of his room, glowing as with fire in the reflected light from the west. The ancient signboard creaked in the gusty night-wind. Fog blew in from the sea, beading upon her jacket, making little jewels on her long lashes and in her hair, cool upon her cheek.

She rode into St. Bruno. Impulsively, at Marc Duclos' gate she dismounted and led Feu Follet up to the door. Marc's car, always muddy and battered, was parked by the side entrance. He himself opened the door just as she lifted the brass-knocker. She saw gladness in his dark face, in his tired eyes that, however long denied the bliss of closing in slumber, never lost their brightness.

He took her hand reverently, drew her into the hall.

FOG OVER FUNDY

"I am so glad you have come." He did not look at her when he spoke. "I have been miserable, gnawing my knuckles and wearing out the pattern of my rug, ever since this morning. What a fool you must have thought me, and a poor sort of fellow to boot! I was mad. I guess it was the peasant in me cropping out. Now I have had time to think, I am very contrite. I shall be glad of even a little of your friendship, Armande. Glad — I do not say what I mean."

"But I think I know." A little smile curved her lips, a fond smile: he was so young, so terribly earnest.

"And I — I do wish you happiness — with him."

"Thank you, Marc. It took a brave man and a good one to say that. But I came to tell you that you misunderstood. It was goodby you saw — only goodby. After all, he loved me in his fashion: I kissed him."

"You — you are not going to marry him! But I thought —"

"I am not going to marry him, Dr. Duclos. And I'm not going to stand here and explain why, because, possibly, I don't know. And don't gloat, Marc. I can see you are raised to the seventh heaven."

LITANY

"Oh, Armande, I am so glad." He bit his lip, forced back a rush of speech. "Come. I shall give you tea."

"Only a cigarette; then I must go." They went into his study and sat on either side of the fire. He lighted a cigarette for her and himself smoked a pipe, hands clasped in front of him, gazing now at her, now at the flames, too happy for words.

"Today," she said musingly, "I have quarrelled with everyone, first Roger, then you, then Ulric. After a fashion, I made peace with Roger; with you, I have made a lasting peace, *n'est-ce pas?*"

"Yes. It was all my fault. I was a prig, an idiot, to act so. What right had I—"

"Some right, I think. I could not be angry with you, Marc. Ulric and I had a great battle."

"Because you told him you were not going to marry Lavergne?"

"Largely. I do not see how I can make peace with Ulric." She looked despondently into the glowing masses of rock-maple. "I shall be glad when Leon comes."

"He is coming then? When?"

FOG OVER FUNDY

"Soon, I hope. He is in New York. Roger saw him there. I feel uneasy about him. It is foolish, I know. One never knows where he is or what he is doing. But that he should be so near home and not write — "

"He wished to surprise you. That is it. He will arrive any time. I know Leon. I too shall be glad to see him back home. I hope he will stay this time."

"He must stay. Ulric has let things go to the devil up there. Cobwebs and must and mold — not literally, you know. But there is a canker eating at the spirit of the place — and it was a good place. It breaks my heart to see it going down, like a fine man ruined by his own weakness and leaving himself a prey to disease. The stone foundations of a good house may crumble and decay, but when its soul becomes tainted — "

"Taint could never be in you, Armande. I sometimes think you should have been a nun."

"I assure you I have never felt nunlike, Marc, *mon vieux*. If you persist in going through life idealizing women, putting them up on pedestals and chanting litanies to them, I fear you are in for some bad times. I thought doctors had no illusions like that."

LITANY

"But I have known you, you see."

"La-la!" She stood up, laughing. "You are hopeless. You are very dear. You are very kind to me. I must go now. Soon we shall meet again, now we are at peace?"

"Soon." He took her hand and raised it to his lips and kissed it lightly. He looked at her bravely enough now. "There is no pedestal high enough on which to place you; no litany sweet enough to say to you. The litany of my love says only over and over again, Armande — 'I love you! I love you!'"

CHAPTER IV

MISERERE

THE spired hills were darkening against the western sky when Armande rode up the driveway to Beausejour. The shadows of the tall cedars lengthened on the grass and a strange stillness seemed to brood over the gray towers. It was more than the stillness of evening, a deeper, profounder hush that seemed to enter into her spirit and drive away all lesser things leaving only an expectant wonder, a question that, though she did not know its answer, filled her with something akin to dread.

She left Feu Follet with young Hervé, the stable-boy, and walked slowly around again to the front of the house. The silence irked her. Why was there no chirping of birds, no fluttering of wings from the dovecote, no bark from Sirdar or from Ulric's black St.

MISERERE

Hubert's in the kennels behind the house. She felt like shouting, like banging doors or upsetting one of the huge wooden-rockers on the colonnaded porch.

Ulric came out as she climbed the steps. There in the shadows she could not see his face clearly, only the great bulk of him against the black cavern of the open door, and the spread of his legs. "*Nom de Dieu*, what has happened to this place, Ulric?" She drew off her hat wearily and laid it with her gloves and riding-crop on the wide white balustrade. "One would think it was the abode of the seven sleepers. If a pin dropped it would sound like thunder. And you—" She stared at him in the dusk — "have you lost your voice, you who had so much of it this afternoon?"

"I—" Ulric choked. "Armande—Armande—"

"What is it?" She strode towards him, seized his arm angrily, her eyes, bright with impatience, looked close into his.

"Leon!" he said hoarsely. "Leon—"

"What of Leon? Not — not anything—?"

"Dead!" Ulric's lips twitched. She felt the tremor of his body as she let go his arm. She did not move away

FOG OVER FUNDY

from him. They stood close together, face-to-face, brother and sister now, more perhaps than they had ever been before or ever would be again.

" I received a telegram from New York, from Paul Carrier, who used to fly with Leon. It was rather vague. Leon was found in some hunting lodge in the mountains. He had been shot. He had been there for some days — "

" It was this woman," said Armande slowly.

" No doubt. Paul did not say. The place belonged to a man named Dumont — Michael Dumont. The message was meagre. But they are sending the body on here. Tomorrow night he — it will be here."

" Leon — ! " Suddenly Armande turned from him and her shoulders drooped and her body shook with weeping terrible to see. Ulric lifted his arms helplessly as if he would take her to him and console her, but he could not, and he knew she did not want it. She dropped into a chair and her fingers, so white in the gloom, raked the luminous ripples of her hair. Her sobbing ceased abruptly and she sat, elbows on knees, staring out upon the darkening reaches of the Tantramar, thinking of days that had been bright, seeing Leon as of old, home

MISERERE

from college, home from the wars; a boy one day, a man the next, red-headed, blue-eyed, tall and straight, filled with the joy of life, impatient of anything that savored of slowness or sorrow. And now this homecoming —

"Strange," she said at last, "that only today I should have spoken of his return, and wished for it so much; and all the time I thought of it, and talked of it — We must know who did this. The one must be punished. Leon — to survive a thousand deaths in battle, to dare a thousand more, then to meet the end like this — in some wretched place, by some unworthy hand — "

"It is a terrible thing," said Ulric. His voice quavered and sounded as if he, too, were on the point of weeping, but Armande knew suddenly that whatever grief he felt was small, was negligible almost, compared with something else that might have been relief. She thought, and despised herself for thinking so, that this homecoming of Leon's was perhaps more welcome to Ulric than one which would have seen Leon quick with the old life, ready to jolt him out of the rut into which he had settled.

FOG OVER FUNDY

"You have told no one else?"

"Oh, yes. I called Marc Duclos, thinking you might be there. You had gone. I told Marc. I have wired to our uncle and to Aunt Sophie and to Aunt Melusine and to some other near friends of our family. Also to Roger Lavergne."

"He will not have reached home."

"To Quebec City I wired. He will return." Armande fancied that Ulric looked at her hopefully, thinking perhaps that in her grief and loneliness, she would turn to Roger. Perhaps she did Ulric wrong to think so. Surely he was not so crass as to let his hopes of her marrying well intrude upon this hour.

"I have talked too, with Père Archambeault. The funeral will be Thursday morning."

"Yes." Armande nodded dully. "Yes, the funeral. Black banners and muffled drums and voices singing the Libera and the Miserere — 'Have pity upon me, have pity upon me, at least you, my friend, for the Hand of the Lord hath touched me.' The catafalque and the death-tapers and a yawning hole in the ground and earth rattling on the wood of the box —"

MISERERE

"Stop it! Stop it, I say!" Ulric's big hand descended on her shoulder. He shook her roughly. "You talk like a madwoman. You are hysterical —"

"No, Ulric —" Her voice had been calm, still was — "I am not hysterical. I am just seeing it all as it will be. The end of life for Leon — he was so young, Leon — so strong, so — well, one did not think of death in connection with him."

"He lived with Death," said Ulric harshly. "Walked with it, flew with it, slept with it. He held Death in fine contempt."

"Do not you?"

Ulric's mouth opened to answer, but he could not answer.

"I thought," continued Armande softly, "that it was characteristic of our family — to count life as little and death as less."

"One need not be a fool," blustered Ulric. "There is such a thing as common-sense and — and reason —"

"Oh, yes," nodded Armande, "common-sense and reason." She stood up, took her hat, gloves and riding-crop from the balustrade. "I shall go to my room now.

FOG OVER FUNDY

I shall not meet you at dinner, Ulric. Only you and I to sit at the long table now — only you and I and a few ghosts."

Ulric's teeth clicked angrily. " I wish you would not talk like that. I swear you'd give a man the creeps. Ghosts — I do not believe in ghosts. Anyway, if there were such, why should one be afraid of them? "

" I am not afraid." She paused as she passed in front of him. " In fact, I should welcome their presence. They would be kindly ghosts to me. Perhaps sometimes they could take me by the hand as my father did when I was very little, and as Leon did; and hold my hand when my steps were none too sure. Have you ever felt the need of one to take your hand, Ulric, one who is strong and fearless and in whose strength and fearlessness you could trust? "

Ulric shook his head. He did not follow her. He was tired, jittery, his system shouted for stimulant. He followed Armande into the hall. She mounted the great stairway; he shambled along to the library. He thought exultantly, putting in a hypocritical sigh of grief, that now he would be undisturbed, that now no Leon could

MISERERE

come to usurp his place and upset the alcoholic tenor of his days. Armande was a silly young girl. Now surely, when a respectable time had elapsed, she would marry Roger Lavergne, go off to Montreal with him to live and leave Ulric and Beausejour in peace. The way looked bright and clear for Ulric.

He filled his glass and lifted it to drink to his happiness, but suddenly recollecting the occasion he put on a sad face, said, "Poor Leon. It is very sad indeed. A great blow," and drank a bit more slowly. He felt better. He began to tell himself he really was pretty well cut up over Leon, that he'd thought a great deal of Leon and that Armande didn't understand him if for one moment she thought that he didn't feel Leon's loss a great deal more than she did. He began to shed tears presently and to feel very lonely. When Père Archambeault, the curé, came, Ulric was a picture of grief and brokenly accepted the good priest's condolences.

Through the evening Marc Duclos called, and Lorenzo Frenette, the notary, and some others of the village-leaders, to proffer their sympathy. Ulric took it all. Armande did not leave her room, and when, after all

FOG OVER FUNDY

had gone, Ulric came there and knocked, her voice, low and clear, told him to go away.

"But you should have put in an appearance!" he said. "What way is that to act! What do you do, sitting there alone in the darkness?"

"I watch the stars, Ulric; the millions and millions of little stars and think how far away they are, and how this earth too is just a little pinpoint of light, and we who live on it—"

"I should think, my girl," said Ulric majestically, "it would be more fitting to meditate upon death and to pray for your brother's soul, rather than sit stargazing."

He waited a while for an answer. When none came he went along to his own room, had a final nightcap and turned in. He started a prayer for Leon, got bogged in the middle, gave it up and soon was snoring peacefully. Armande heard his noisy grunting when she passed his door a little later. She could not stay in the house tonight. Perhaps tomorrow night when Leon was here, when he lay sleeping in the wavering light of the tapers, she would sit beside him. But not tonight. There was

MISERERE

only one place to take her sorrow tonight. With only the stars to light her path, she crossed the fields and followed the great dike, walking along the path on its rim, down to the sea.

The salt wind was cool on her cheek and in the vasty vault of heaven sprinkled so lavishly with milky light and in the great mystery of the waters, in their murmurous voices, was some peace, some sublime consolation such as could never come from man. Here, long after midnight, while all the world about her slept, she stood, gazing out to sea, lonely as the shadowy gulls whose wing-beats sounded softly above her. Here Death did not seem so terrible nor Life so precious; here one caught glimpses of eternity, of all the ages the world has been, of all the endless ages it will be. And slowly, reverently, as a devout worshipper from some great shrine, she left the dikes and the sea and the sky with a great calm in her spirit, with hope and love and pity.

From the white portico of Beausejour, this glittery Autumn morning, the dark procession moved off, following the mortal remains of Leon de Vysart to the

FOG OVER FUNDY

church and cemetery of St. Bruno. Many old friends of the family were there: dignified doctors, lawyers and politicians. Then, with faded ribbons on shabby coats, walked a small detail of men who had known Leon in the brave young days of the war. Dr. Marc Duclos was there, walking stiffly with Roger Lavergne, and there was a military uncle, General Hippolyte de Vysart, who, with the two aunts now riding in the family limousine with Armande, had come all the way from Ottawa.

Armande sat, pale, big-eyed, silent, between the ramrod stiffness of Aunt Sophie and the cushioned plumpness of Aunt Melusine. Lack of sleep and utter indifference to food, had told little on Armande, serving only to make her loveliness more spiritual and appealing. She had spent long hours at Leon's side, not gazing much at the chiselled handsome face, in death almost clear of the harsh markings of war and dissipation. She did not need to look in that face to recall the boy that had been and she preferred to think of him in her own way, to see the image in her heart, treasured there since she was a little girl and he her god.

MISERERE

Now down the leafy lanes and across the marsh between the ramparts of the dikes, now through the rumbling covered-bridge over the gleaming river and into the winding street, the sad procession passed, until it reached the tall-spired church. There the long box was borne by stalwart comrades into the cool gloom, and soft voices began the eerily beautiful chant of the Office for the Dead.

The windows were hung with black drapes and against the walls were banners of sable velvet on which were inscribed the words of the scriptures — *Memini mei saltem vos amici mei* — the words that Armande had spoken to Ulric there in the dusk when the news of Leon's passing had reached her — "Have pity upon me, have pity upon me, at least you, my friends, for the Hand of the Lord hath touched me."

Now came the curé in black chausable and the thurifers and the bearer of the holy water in its silvern dish. Now up to the open rail in the high altar the bier was carried and set down among the tall guttering tapers in black candle-sticks. From the choir loft into the solemn stillness, as the priest began the mass, drifted the poign-

FOG OVER FUNDY

antly beautiful music and still more beautiful words of the Mass for the Dead, and filled the church with a myriad sounds of grieving and lamentation mingled with joy in the great mercy of God and exultation in His goodness —

> Eternal rest grant to him, O Lord
> And let perpetual light shine upon him.
>
> .   .   .   .   .
>
> O Lord, hear my prayer.
> And let my cry come unto Thee.

Armande and her aunts, in decent black, knelt in the front pew on one side of the bier; Ulric and General Hippolyte, huger still than Ulric, were in the corresponding pew on the other side. In the pew behind them knelt, side-by-side, Roger Lavergne, millionaire newspaper-proprietor, a blue-blood of New France, knight-commander-elect, and Marc Duclos, humble doctor of medicine from the Sorbonne, son of a long line of peasants, builders of dikes and tillers of the soil — the two of them akin in one thing only — their love for the slender girl whose pale gleaming hair showed more

MISERERE

strikingly, in contrast with the black of the little felt hat from under whose brim it crept in waves of beauty.

They prayed to God, these two, somewhat mechanically perhaps, to have mercy upon the soul of the faithful departed, but in their hearts was a deeper, more fervent prayer for her, that she might find great joy, that this sorrow should pass from her, that to them, to one of them, it should be given to guard and protect her, the one with his wealth and power, the other with his loyalty and strength. All about them was rustling of whispered prayers; the soft dry sound of chaplets, wooden beads slipping through fingers — soft young fingers, gnarled old fingers, fingers guiltless of stain or mark, fingers cracked and calloused with years of toil — voice upon voice whispering, repeating, insisting — God, have mercy on his soul — God have mercy on his soul — Kyrie eleison — kyrie eleison —

From the choir the mystic minor plaint of the Dies Irae —

> Day of Wrath, that dreadful day
> When heaven and earth shall pass away —

FOG OVER FUNDY

Thus with beauty, with magic of chord and phrase, with the centuries-old ritual that has marked the earthly last of prince and peasant, did Mother Church give its final benediction to the departed soul of Leon de Vysart, and with murmured prayers on the grave's rough edge, that sunny morning, with the happy birds chirping in the churchyard trees and the doves fluttering about their cote above the presbytery's gray slate roof, the senseless clay went back into that whence it had sprung. The earth and rubble showered like shot on the wooden box, swiftly the grave filled up. Armande, with Roger on one side, Marc on the other, walked out of the churchyard and entered the waiting car, in which already her aunts, looking rather like twin spectres with a tomb of their own, were seated.

"Well, child," said stiff-backed Sophie, "it is all over now, and one must be resigned to the will of God — though I do say you have borne up very well under this ordeal. There are only you and Ulric now."

"Yes, only you two," helped Melusine. "Of course we all grieve for Leon. It was the war, no doubt — the war that caused so much confusion among our young,

MISERERE

and broke so many lives. Now you and Ulric must be all-in-all to each other —"

Her voice rumbled on. Armande did not hear. She saw as the car moved off, a woman, one who could not be much older than herself — a woman who held a little boy by the hand. Armande knew the child at once — the curly golden hair, the great blue eyes and the halo of heaven all about the proud little head. The woman's eyes were red with weeping and haunted with grief so real, so terrible, that Armande forgot her own sorrow in its contemplation.

Paul Emil's mother, Suzanne Delagarde, wife of Gregoire the fisherman, who had been drowned — drowned — But why should this peasant-girl weep, careless of who observed her grieving, why should she clutch her little boy by the hand and draw him close to her as the car in which Armande sat went by them? Paul Emil's eyes were wide with wonder, with a faint reflection of the misery in his mother's. But he saw Armande and his face broke into a smile that was like a sunburst after a storm and he waved his hand gaily at her.

FOG OVER FUNDY

She leaned from the window and smiled down at him. "*Holà*, Paul Emil, my brave one," she called softly as she passed abreast of him. Then from the child's face to the mother's she looked with infinite pity and understanding. Suzanne turned away, her eyes averted sullenly, as if she resented any encroachment upon her sorrow, as if she resented it most from this woman of the de Vysarts.

"I declare, Armande," said Sophie peevishly, "you have not been listening to me at all."

"No, *ma tante*."

"But you should listen! There are matters on which Melusine and I can advise you."

"Such as?" Armande, with an effort, forced herself to listen, while Sophie's sharp tones cut into one ear and Melusine's rumbled syllables rolled into the other.

"Sophie," said Melusine, "was speaking of marriage."

"But surely Aunt Sophie is not going to marry —"

"How dare you!" Sophie's shoulder bored into Armande's. "Are you being purposely frivolous? I, marry!

MISERERE

Why ever should I marry? It is of your marriage I wish to speak."

"But I am not—"

"Of course you are. A blind person could see that Sir Roger Lavergne adores you—"

"He is not Sir Roger yet, Sophie," pointed out Melusine. "Not until after New Year's."

"Well, he is as good as. Anyway, don't quibble, Melusine. I dare say it will be next year—in June doubtless, that you and he—"

"Oh, no," said Armande. "I think not."

"You think not!" Both aunts stared at her. Their stares were overpowering. "Child," bumbled Melusine, "you do not know what you are saying. No girl ever had a finer chance than you have. A fortune, a title, a high-place in society—"

"It's your bounden duty, Armande," said Sophie. "I cannot for a moment believe that this—er—refusal of yours is anything but a manifestation of maidenly shyness. Very fitting, of course, very proper—and it does you honor. One must not seem to be too eager about such things. But with me and Melusine you do not need to pretend."

"I will not, if you please, talk about it now," said Armande pleadingly. "I — there is much to think about right now."

"Oh, very well." Sophie looked primly at her sister. "I really do not know what girls are coming to nowadays. Why, in my time — "

"Yes, aunt," murmured Armande. She caught the eye of young Hervé, who was driving, and looked at him so urgently that with sudden pressure on the pedal, he made the big car leap from a crawl to a dash, so that very shortly they were back at Beausejour and there was no more talk of marriage.

In the drawing-room some dozen of the mourners were solemnly drinking sherry and eating biscuits. When Armande came there, Roger brought her a glass and put it in her hand. "Drink this, Armande, for me. I know how little you have slept and eaten. That is no good. But this has been cruel for you."

"Crueller perhaps for some others."

"What do you mean? What others? Ulric — ?"

MISERERE

"Ulric does not care." They both looked at Ulric, busy with the sherry and General Hippolyte, also a great authority on dogs and horses.

"Then who else?" persisted Roger.

Armande shook her head. She sipped the amber wine and took a biscuit from the tray Roger held out to her. "What about this man who — who killed Leon?"

"They will find him eventually. This girl, Iris Wayland, with whom Leon was so intimate, swears that she left Leon and Michael Dumont together at this place, Sunset Lodge. Dumont disappeared that day. There is no trace of him. But a man cannot vanish like that — not in these days of lightning communication. They will find him and make him talk. It was in his place it happened, it was his pistol, and he was engaged to this Wayland girl and very much in love with her. It is, the papers say, a clear case of jealousy. Dumont had been away; he always allowed the woman to use his lodge. He went there by chance and found her with Leon. She says there was nothing between her and Leon, and I believe it. But Dumont could not know that — "

"This woman — ?"

FOG OVER FUNDY

"A show-girl. Dumont was wild about her."

"He must have been," said Armande pensively, "if he would — kill for her. But she — does she not defend his action? Did she not love him?"

"Who can say?" Roger shrugged. "But she cannot defend him. They quarrelled in the lodge. She said she would not stay. She had her own car and went back in it to New York, leaving Leon and Dumont there. She says Dumont called her that night and said that everything was all right between him and Leon, but that he was going away. That was why she did not worry about Leon and did not think anything was wrong until they found — That was days after."

"I will not think of it, Roger. It is done — forever done; and what happens after, what they do to these people whom I have never seen, and never wish to see, is no concern of mine. When first I heard of this, of what had happened to Leon, I thought of an eye for an eye. I do not think so now. I do not care."

"You would not wish to see this man hanged for what he did, for the crime of murder!"

Armande shook her head. "I do not know. Perhaps,

MISERERE

yes. It is a cruel thing to take a life — "

"And you loved Leon."

"I loved him very much."

"Well then! You must feel no pity or softness towards his slayer. I shall use all my power, all the resources I command, to find this man and bring him to the death-house. I loved Leon too. He was young to die. With him, perhaps with this woman, it was an innocent enough flirtation."

"Leon was good and noble," said Armande stoutly. "He would harm no one."

"But jealousy —" Roger thought of the morning on the rim of the Devil's Cauldron — "will make a man say and do strange things." He gazed across the room at Dr. Marc Duclos, sandwiched between the macabre aunts. "What more of the stranger at the White Roe?"

"No more. I dare say he will be up and away about his business shortly. They found some of those who were drowned, and some matchwood — all that the rocks had left of the yacht."

"It is a grim country, this. Death seems always so

imminent. Why not come to Montreal this winter, Armande; my sisters would welcome you, and I — well, I do not need to say what it would mean to me. Won't you come?"

"Thank you, no. There is more reason than ever now for my staying at home. I had hoped, you see — that — that Leon would be here, that he could wake Beausejour and Ulric from their lethargy. Now it is up to me."

Roger looked at her with pity and adoration. "Up to you — so frail, so fine, to pit your strength against a land that it took generations of horny-handed peasants to subdue; up to you to sustain the fortunes of a house that strong men built. What can you do, Armande?"

"I can fight." Her chin came up proudly and there was bold defiance in the firmness of her mouth, the quick flash of her eyes. "That I can do; that I will do."

"I wish you well. You are brave, fearless — reckless perhaps." He saw no hope for her. He knew, better than she, how far their fortunes had fallen, how weak Ulric was. There was nothing, more than a bare living, that she could get from this ramshackle chateau and the

MISERERE

miles of land around it. But he did not speak of those things, knowing he could not daunt her, not wishing to do anything to spoil her splendid vision.

Presently the company began to separate. General Hippolyte, Aunt Sophie and Aunt Melusine, with enough bags and boxes for a world tour, got into the car to be driven to the railroad-station at Sackville, en route to Upper Canada. Roger, also, made his adieux and Marc, unable to say the words of sympathy and helpfulness that choked him and filled his heart to bursting, said a gruff farewell and followed, in his rickety sedan, the Daimler's shining black and silver streak.

Armande and Ulric, the strong young willow and the great oak with the rotted core, stood on the front steps until all had gone; then, in silence, they went into the house, into the drawing-room where plates and empty wine-glasses told of the departed company, where the noonday sun lay bright on the faded green of the rug and on the faded silver of the wall-paper. Ulric went to the hearth and tapped the dottle from his pipe by striking the bowl against his big palm. He blew

FOG OVER FUNDY

noisily on the stem and loaded the pipe from a porcelain jar that had been his father's. Through the match-flame and the blue gray wisps of smoke he looked apprehensively at Armande. "Well," he ventured, puffing comfortably, "it's all over now."

"Yes — that part of it. But the rest is just beginning."

"What do you mean?"

"I mean that we must work, you and I, to bring the life-blood back into the veins of this place. It's moribund, it's dying right under our noses. *Sapristi!* Ulric, can't you smell the must —"

Ulric snuffed. "I smell no —"

"I do not mean real must. I mean — oh, I will not go on. You must see that the place is going to ruin. Stir yourself, can't you! We have the richest farmlands in the Tantramar —"

"No money in farming," mumbled Ulric uneasily.

"There's no money in anything until one tries to get it. We have to try."

"But you — why should you be so concerned about — about this? All you have to do is say the word —"

MISERERE

"To Roger Lavergne? It will never be said, Ulric. My destiny is here — in this house, in this land. Here I belong. Here I stay. Mind you that, big Ulric, and if you cherish any hopes of my getting out, of my swapping tweeds for silks and a saddle for cushions, you are a bigger fool than I think."

Ulric savagely rubbed his mane. "God deliver me! God save me from such a witch! I'll not, I tell you, be hagridden by you, Armande. I'll not!" He was terribly glad that Leon could never now come to stand by her side and lend his great strength to hers. Bah! She was only a girl, small, frail — What could she do?

"Ulric," she said so softly that he jumped, "this place is going to live again. If you won't work with me, then I shall have to work alone. But I must know from you very soon how we stand. I have never talked to you of money. I have asked little and I got it. But now I must know."

"Why — why, what would you know about? Things like that, business matters, are not for young girls like you. I've told you and I tell you again; marry, marry Roger, get a house and family of your own. Then you

FOG OVER FUNDY

can run it to your heart's content. But you can't run me, vixen. I won't — won't have it! "

"You'll have it, Ulric. And you'll like it. I have my say here, you know. Do what I bid you. As the bible says, dear Ulric, 'Give an account of thy stewardship.' If you won't, I shall have to go to Monsieur Frenette, a most astute lawyer — "

"Don't you! Don't you dare to — to drag the affairs of our family out into the light of day and — "

"Won't they bear scrutiny? What do you fear?"

For answer, Ulric strode out of the room, his lips moving, but no sound issuing therefrom. Armande stood by the big window, feeling her loneliness, feeling the helplessness she would never admit. Her mouth trembled and her eyes misted, but resolutely she stilled the one and from the others shook away the clouding mist. There in the noonday stillness of the old house, it came to her with all its cruel implications, that she was the last of her line, that Ulric could not be counted upon. The last — Her lips parted and her eyes widened at the thought, the sudden remembrance of the little golden-

MISERERE

haired boy, Paul Emil; of that peasant-girl's tear-swollen eyes.

"But no," she said softly. "Leon was good and noble. Leon would harm no one."

From the spire of St. Bruno's church, far-off, borne to her on the keen sea-wind clearly, came the sonorous clanging of the bell — the Angelus, and she bent her head bright in the yellow sunlight and murmured as a child would murmur —

"Behold the handmaid of the Lord;
Be it done unto me according to Thy word."

CHAPTER V

THE WITCH AND THE PEASANT

THE Autumn's gorgeous cloak was faded and tattered and the bare bones of the tall white and yellow birch, the starkness of beech and maple loomed darkly against the gray November sky. The last legions of the wild geese had gone their southward way and only the echo of their lonely honking seemed to linger over the marshlands. In the mornings the thick hoar-frost glistened on the dun-colored grass and at night shone with a myriad diamond-points under the sky. The timid deer slipped from the forest's edge and haunted the orchards seeking the few apples left to freeze upon the bough. The flowers on Leon de Vysart's grave had long since withered and been scattered by the whistling blasts.

The two weeks following the funeral, Armande stayed at home, taking long walks over the fields with

THE WITCH AND THE PEASANT

Sirdar and Nicanor, one of Ulric's black St. Hubert's that she liked better than the others. Ulric himself went off to the Miramichi Country to hunt moose, having made rendezvous there with General Hippolyte de Vysart, a mighty Nimrod. Ulric made no bones about leaving Armande alone. She might, he told her slyly, take a trip to Montreal: the change would do her good, but he did not insist when she refused. During the second week of his absence a fine hind-quarter of moose arrived and shortly afterward a note, execrably written, saying he would be home soon.

Armande knew that he stayed away so long in order to postpone any talk of business. He hoped, perhaps, that she would forget all about their disagreement and let things go on their old lackadaisical course. He did not know Armande. Left to her own devices, she went over every yard of ground they possessed, into every farm and cottage, every cow-byre and stable, noting everywhere the havoc that neglect and indifference had wrought, seeing the holes through which their wealth had trickled. She spent long evenings alone before the library fire making notes of the day's observations, making count-

FOG OVER FUNDY

less memoranda that she knew, with sinking heart, would bewilder Ulric and have him all at sea before he had read a dozen of them. From the provincial Department of Agriculture she procured such booklets as were available on the raising of bacon-hogs and poultry, easily the two most profitable branches of stock-breeding in a region so close to the seaports directly in contact with the great buying power of the Old Country.

It was all very fascinating, even to her, born and bred upon the land. She had never liked the cities, never been able to comprehend how people could live cooped up in narrow houses in narrow streets with smoke for a sky and the vile fumes exhaled by motors filling the air they breathed. Here in the Tantramar one could live, one could stretch, one could find the cool beauty of the dawn and the warm glory of the sunset. One could walk beneath the moon that mellowed the marshes with its blue and silver light.

This night there was a moon, floating full and free over the distant hills. Armande put out the green shaded light on the library table, left her books and papers and stood in the bow-window revelling in the witchery that

THE WITCH AND THE PEASANT

transformed barn and haycock and dike into things of enchantment, that made shadows of deep dark velvet upon the lawn, that made the frost gleam and jewel with wondrous lights.

She loved this solitude. It was almost midnight now; the servants had long ago retired, and in all the cottages and farmsteads on the borders of the Tantramar no light shone. It was good, somehow, to be awake when all the world lay sleeping. It seemed as if, then, all the beauty was for one's self alone. All this was hers, though gladly she would have shared it, had there been any to share it with.

Perhaps Marc Duclos, a night-hawk like herself, would still be sitting in front of his fire, poring over one of his eternal books on anatomy or some such tedious thing. Marc had been away for a week, his annual holiday, tramping through the beautiful land of Cocagne with a stick instead of a gun. He would be home now, but she did not want to go to him, to see that look of worship and wonder in his eyes. Had he loved her less, she would have liked him more; had he hated her, perhaps she would have loved him. As it was, she felt guilty in his presence and knew her own unworthiness, her inability to measure up to the superhuman ideas he had of her. Yes, she thought fondly of Marc tonight — Marc so utterly loyal, so strong and trustworthy. And she wondered if there was something lacking in her, who could no more respond to these splendid virtues in him than she could to Roger Lavergne's suavity, his brilliant intellect and handsome looks.

"Perhaps," she mused to the moon, "it is as Marc said: I should have been a nun and spent my days in the cloister — Soeur Armande de la croix. I would be a pale little nun, and with all my hair shorn off, how droll I would look. Then, one day while I was on promenade, I would see a horse and, presto, I should vault upon his back, robes and all and bring eternal scandal upon the community. No, no — not a nun. Just because one cannot love, must one be a nun? If that is so, heyday, the world must be full of nuns. But why do I waste time here!"

Presently, with long easy steps, Armande walked down the drive in the shadow of the cedars, then out upon the highroad lying wide and white in the moon-

THE WITCH AND THE PEASANT

light. Gaily she marched along, singing softly now, again speaking to her faithful shadow, stopping now and then to gaze at the marshes and the river and the distant sea, to breathe deeply and to smile with sheer content.

Thus she came to St. Bruno's Church, passed under the lych-gate and walked up to the chancel door, gazing upon the white tombstones and the crosses that stood at crazy angles in the half-frozen ground, stopping for a moment at the fenced-in plot dominated by a great white marble cross, where the de Vysarts were buried, where a new mound reared itself for a while above the sunken sward but soon would go down to the level of the rest.

Because often she played the organ for the curé, she was allowed a key of her own. She used it now and entered, climbing the narrow stairs to the choir-loft, her way lighted by the moonbeams of blue, green, gold and scarlet that filtered through the robes of St. Catherine with her wheel and Patrick with his crozier, that fell athwart aisle and pew and chancel rail and came

FOG OVER FUNDY

through the oriel high above her in a burst of prismatic light.

For a while she sat on the organ-bench hearing the rustling sounds of the night in the draughty dimness of the old church — the tapping of dead branches against the window-panes, the creak of ancient floor-boards trodden perhaps by some ghostly passenger, the scurrying of mice beneath the choir-floor. She could see, through the side-window the spectral shapes of the tombstones in the churchyard; see, far beyond, the silvered waters of the bay, the moonlit, silent marshlands and the shadowy walls of the dikes.

She thought of her life, so wild and free of old, into which now had come some purpose, some serious trend that made her feel as if she had passed in the road a certain milestone beyond which the way was rougher and more exacting and one had to walk more warily and take thought of all that lay about. She thought of the life of the cities where she had spent a part of each year, of how, sheltered and bulwarked by wealth and position, she could dwell there secure, needing to take no thought of what life might mean, of where happiness

THE WITCH AND THE PEASANT

lay, of what constituted the heart's content. A pleasant, opiate existence such as thousands of other women led. A home, a family, a husband; the years dropping by with a pleasant, deadly sameness; the ashen hair fading to gray, to white, the cheek withering, the eye losing its brightness. No more the sea-wind salt and stinging in her face, no more the lash of rain or the bite of frost, the miry roads in spring, the flamboyant glory of the Autumn —

Not for her, who loved each day for what of beauty it might give; not for her whose reaching finger-tips could touch the golden clouds above the hills of Acadia, whose flying tresses felt the caress of sun and shower. She could not be uprooted from this soil, this land, of which she was a part — never uprooted to be taken away, to fade, to wither, to die in some place beyond sight and sound of the things she loved so warmly.

Softly she played, idly, sweetly; dulcet haunting reedy tones like elfin voices there in the sacred quiet of St. Bruno's Church; strange, eery music that so often by night floated from the gray ivied walls to the ears of some belated peasant, who, hearing it, crossed him-

FOG OVER FUNDY

self piously and, murmuring a prayer to the Virgin and to good St. Bruno, hurried faster along the white ribbon of road and shiveringly fancied that trolls and witches and creatures strange to see lurked behind every dike and every row of willows. "The White Witch sat last night at the organ," one would say to the gaping audience in the market-place or the post-office or in the parlor of the White Roe. "And it didn't sound like earthly music at all. Père Archambeault should exorcise that one. Surely she plays for wild spirits like her own that come up out of the sea and out of the graveyard to join hands and dance their evil dances about the House of God."

But they dared not speak of these things in her hearing nor bring their fears to the gray-haired curé, who had no patience with believers in witch-craft, who worked ceaselessly to eradicate the lingering poison of the pagan beliefs his flock had inherited from their remote ancestors of La Manche, from many a Norman and Breton fireside where talk of witches and goblins flourished.

Armande played in a world alone, a world of beauti-

THE WITCH AND THE PEASANT

ful sound, of gorgeous colored harmony. Now the music swelled in a crashing crescendo, now faded to the softness of waters upon smooth pebbles or wind among the birches. Then, gradually, she came out of that world of dream, was drawn out of it by the slow-creeping consciousness of eyes that watched her. She did not stop playing, though her fingers moved slower over the keys. She gazed into the mirror above the organ and saw there a shadow, saw the pallor of its face in the moonlight. Still she played softly and still more softly; then suddenly she said, "Who are you? And what do you wish?"

For a moment there was no answer. She desisted, swung around on the bench and stared at the intruder, standing there in a shaft of light. Solitary, strange and forlorn he looked; almost as forlorn as when she had gazed upon his white, sea-bleached face pressed against the window of the White Roe on that night of wind and storm.

"John Gower, seaman, is it not?" she said.

"Yes." He had a blue cap crushed in his hand. She saw the thick black waves of his hair above the still

FOG OVER FUNDY

pallid face. " Yes, that is it. And you — you are the girl — that girl — "

" I am Armande de Vysart."

" Yes — Armande. I have thought of you. Once I saw you pass the inn on horseback. You ride bravely. And you are brave. I can realize now what you did for me that night — and I a stranger, with no claim upon you. I wish I could repay you, but — "

"Yes, but — ? "

" But you impress one as being the kind of person to whom no repayment is possible or necessary. You play like the muse herself. I was walking along the road in the moonlight, thinking perhaps I could find by moonlight a road I've not been able to find by day. Then, as I passed this old church I stopped to gaze at it and admire, and I heard music — such music — like sounds from heaven. It seemed supernatural. It gave me a start, I tell you. But it was so lovely. Then I came to see who it was. I did not dream it would be you. I dreamt of you as a spirit of the storm, riding like a Valkyrie through that night of hellish tempest, and I find you sitting at an organ in the dead of night. You

THE WITCH AND THE PEASANT

make me wonder if you are real? If you are not just something in a dream that I am living."

Armande smiled. "You are a fanciful sort of person. I am very real, I think." She slid from the bench. "I must go now. Come. I have to lock the door."

Silent, he followed her down the narrow stairs and out into the shadow and light of the churchyard. He waited while she fastened the door, then walked beside her down the flagged path. At the gate she stopped, looked at him curiously.

"Your road lies that way — " She waved towards the White Roe. "Mine is in the other direction."

John Gower shook his head. "My way is — well, let me go yours for a while, please. I have been out only a few times. I do not know anyone here. At the inn they speak mostly French, which I do not understand very well. The doctor — I have seen him a few times. No one else. I hoped you would come again."

"But Isaac Proux said you threatened to throw visitors out of the window. And when I did go to see you — "

FOG OVER FUNDY

"I suffered for that — afterward. For speaking so to you, but I — "

"You were not well. I know. I understand. It was the shock and your own injuries; the loss of your comrades — "

"Yes, yes; all those things — and more. I felt as if I had been catapulted from another planet."

"Are we so strange a people then?" Armande walking beside him, turned her head and smiled at him. "And is this lovely land so unlike your own?"

"This?" He shook his head. "This place is like heaven. Peace — there is peace everywhere, and quiet and content. There is no evil here."

"But yes, my friend," Armande chided. "It is still part of the world, you know; and we who live here are but human. We have human failings and suffer from human ills. We have doctors, lawyers, priests and, yes, a sturdy jail in St. Bruno, though to be sure it is little used."

"You live here all the time?"

"This is my home. I was born here. For years I came and went. School. Convent. Some travel. I live here now

THE WITCH AND THE PEASANT

with my brother Ulric, in that house you see so dark against the sky up there upon the hill."

"Yes. I know your house. I asked the inn-keeper about you. I was curious. You see, apart from Doctor Duclos, you are the only one I — well, the only one who was good to me. I do not say what I mean," he finished miserably. "I cannot tell you — "

"Perhaps I know."

They walked on, saying nothing, two under the moon, past the sleeping farmsteads, greeted now and then by the echoing bark, clear in the night, of some wakeful collie. Familiarly, their shadows moved side-by-side in the white of the road. The smell of sea and salt-marsh was in their nostrils and the quiet peace and beauty of the night in their hearts.

"This is a bit of heaven," said John Gower. "Strange that I should be walking along this road with you, that I should be here, that it should seem so right for me to be here."

"But you will go away soon? Now you are well?"

"Go away!" His dark eyes studied her almost with surprise. "Why, where should I go?"

FOG OVER FUNDY

"You must have a home." Armande looked at him wonderingly. "A home. Friends. A wife."

"A — No," he said decisively. "None of those things."

"But what about Far Rockaway? You see I recall what we read from your pocketbook that night."

"Nothing there. I think I do not want to go there, to go anywhere. One could be content here?"

"But yes!"

"Then why go anywhere else? There is nothing to take me, nothing at all that I know of. There is more here than I know of any place else. More — " He looked suddenly at the proud beauty of her profile, the mystic loveliness of her hair.

"You are a strange man, that the sea has cast up."

"You speak perhaps more truly than you think. I wonder if anything stranger was ever cast upon your shores. But I came to a pleasant land. Tell me, if I stayed here in St. Bruno, could I see you sometimes and talk with you?"

She laughed gaily. "In St. Bruno I am as easily seen

THE WITCH AND THE PEASANT

and talked to as the church-spire or the White Roe on Isaac's signboard."

"But you are sort of the — the lady of the manor, are you not? I should be a shoemaker or carpenter or fisherman or the like — "

"Pouf! What is that? It matters not at all. Kind hearts and coronets, you know. And we de Vysarts, well, perhaps it would be better if we had now a few cobblers, carpenters and fishermen in our family. *Bon!* Here we come to my gateway, M'sieur John Gower of Far Rockaway, New York. And here we say good night. You were kind to walk with me. You have a long way to go to the White Roe."

"You were kind to let me walk with you. Kind — you were — " His eyes held hers, looking frankly, questioningly into hers. "You were kinder than you knew. Good night."

"*Bon soir.*" Impulsively she held out her hand to him and he took it gently for a moment, bowed and turned away. She watched him down the road, a vague figure, somehow unreal and fantastic, like, as he had said, one catapulted from some other planet. A strange young man, she thought, as she walked up the drive, and, this idea of his that he would find content in St. Bruno, that he would stay here — Armande smiled wisely, thinking of the howling gales of winter, the blizzards, the ice, the cold angry crimson skies of evening, the bitter blue or black of the sub-zero days. He would not stay long. A sailor, the sea would call to him again; a dweller in the busy places of the world, those places would draw him away from the vast solitude, the ancient peace of Acadia.

She thought of him when at last she lay snuggled down in the great old four-poster bed in her tower-room. She pictured him walking solitary across the marshes to his lonely room up under the mossy eaves of the White Roe; of the night of storm, she thought, and of Candace and the wild fury and accusation in his eyes. Now, she thought, the fury of accusation had yielded to a sort of bewildered resignation and a dawning hope. What had his life been that he spoke so earnestly of finding peace here and content? There was something about him, some loneliness, something forlorn, that awoke a warm interest and pity in her heart.

THE WITCH AND THE PEASANT

He seemed lost, a stranger among strangers, pathetically grateful to those who showed him even the slightest kindness. It had been touching, his gratitude to her for letting him walk by her side, for talking to him and permitting him to talk.

"Though, come to think of it," meditated Armande, "he did little talking and said nothing about himself. Well, sailors are often lonely men, with few ties ashore. And it may be he has none. Even so, why should he wish to bury himself in the Tantramar unless — unless there is some good and deep-seated reason for it? However, one shall know. In time one gets to know all things. But a cobbler, a carpenter, a fisherman? I think not. Fine hands like his could belong to none of those noble callings, nor, for that matter, to a seaman. He is a puzzle, this John Gower. I'll wager he has given the White Roe something to discuss. If anything can be learned about him, the villagers and the fireside-oracles will surely find it out."

She fell asleep then and dreamed of John Gower coming up out of the sea, green water streaming from his hair and his garments, sea-weed garlanding him —

FOG OVER FUNDY

coming up out of the sea and groping through the rain and blackness towards a glimmering light that was the old ship's lantern hanging under the porch of the White Roe.

A black north wind was blowing wildly across the Tantramar, when she awoke, driving wisps of faded grass and showers of dry leaves before it, making the dust dance in dervish circles in the road, rattling the window sashes and lashing the bay into wild whitemaned chargers that rushed furiously at the dikes and were shattered into flying spray and spume. The sky was dull and leaden and there was a hint of snow.

From her window she saw a crew of men, directed by Alyre Sormany, the dike-master, one of the ghostly Damase Blais' successors, rebuilding a part of the inner dike, the process varying in no degree from what it had been centuries ago when first this land was reclaimed from the sea. Oxen and horses, huge Clydesdales, were there hauling logs to the scene of operations. The dike was built in the ancient Flemish mode. Rows of trees were set out entire, five or six deep, and between the rows logs were piled lengthwise one atop the other,

THE WITCH AND THE PEASANT

every interstice, every crack and cranny was packed hard then with clay and soon there stood a sea-wall that the Fundy tides might attack in vain. An *essaie*, or flood-gate, set in the dike, allowed the marsh-water to drain off at low tide, but closed automatically against the inrush of the sea at flood.

How strong the dikes were! How like the people — sturdy, stolid, rugged, immutable; the men working from dawn till dark in the fields, the women busy with their invariably large families, yet finding ample time to weave and knit and spin. Having their happy hours too in the frozen evenings beside the roaring wood-stove or the blazing hearth, singing the ancient folk-songs and roundelays that had crossed the stormy seas to echo as sweetly over the hills and marshes of Acadia as they had in the orcharded land of Normandy.

Armande, watching the dike-builders, began to notice one, taller, more agile than the rest. She marked the darkness of his hair contrasting with the blonde and bleached polls of the Acadians. She stared intently. " Why, it is! " She said. " He loses no time, that man. And surely he is a glutton for work to try his hand,

FOG OVER FUNDY

first-off, at dike-building, to match his strength with men like Alyre Sormany and the Malenfants and Cormiers. I can imagine the sweat standing out on that white brow of his. I shall go there."

In short order she was dressed, had partaken of the morning coffee and *brioches,* had watched young Hervé saddle Feu Follet and went riding gaily down the drive and along the paddy-road leading to the marsh where the dike-builders were at work. She reined in Feu Follet and stopped to watch them, acknowledging the awkward salutes of the dike-master and his men, letting her eyes linger for a moment on John Gower. It was the first time she had really got a good look at him. He was, she saw, of a build and mold infinitely finer than the massive hinds he worked with, but his shoulders were as strong, as broad as theirs and the sleeves of his blue shirt, rolled high, disclosed tapering, muscular arms, bronzed by the sun.

He passed close to her, carrying a spruce pole on his shoulder. He looked up, half-shyly, as if he doubted that last night's episode had been real. Armande's quick smile reassured him. He grinned then. His teeth were

THE WITCH AND THE PEASANT

white and strong. He said, " Good morning, Ma'moiselle de Vysart."

" Good morning, M'sieur John Gower. You were quite in earnest then about becoming cobbler, carpenter or fisherman; you have become a builder of dikes. You like it, *hein?* "

" It's fascinating. The dike-master had breakfast at the inn, you see, and we began to talk and I asked him if there was work for me. So here I am."

" You do well. But I must not keep you from your toil."

He gazed at her steadily for a moment, not answering; then he started, smiled sheepishly and hitched his shoulder to ease the weight of the pole. " Forgive me," he said, " if I seem to stare. I was wondering if you could be as lovely under the sun as you were — under the moon."

" And — ? " She knew she should not lead him on like this. She felt the curious looks of the other men, heard the low-voiced mutter of their talk. But something made her ask, forced her to get from him what her heart hungered for.

FOG OVER FUNDY

"And I find you lovelier. I —" He moistened his lips with his tongue-tip. "There is a moon tonight." He looked at the brown sward at his feet.

"Yes. Yes, there is a moon. Well —" She laughed gaily. "Do not work too hard. Adieu."

"Goodby." She could scarcely hear it as he strode off with the unwieldy pole. She spoke to Feu Follet and rode away. It would not do, she knew, to devote too much attention to the stranger. Already, they would be wondering, speculating, guessing wildly about the why's and wherefore's of his staying in St. Bruno. She herself wondered, yet something, some wise little voice in her heart, told her the reason, and she felt a tumult, an unease in her breast. Of course it was all absurd. What had she to do with this bit of drift, this nobody? And that, to be sure, was what the Tantramar folk would think. She had played a part in his rescue though, and some interest in his welfare was therefore excusable.

It was only a natural interest, she told herself, that anyone would take. It was Christian charity; pity perhaps; but the little voice said something irrelevant about the moonlight and made her angry. She was

THE WITCH AND THE PEASANT

frowning, telling herself not to be absurd, when Marc Duclos' car overtook her as she neared the White Roe. Marc stopped and poked his head out the window. His brown eyes looked tired and he ran his fingers nervously through his hair. He said, "Hello, Armande. How have you been? Ulric is not home yet?"

"Still hunting the moose, Marc. I have been very well thank you. And you? You had a good time at Cocagne?"

"One always has a good time at Cocagne — oysters and lobsters and plenty of good food. It is a man's country. I returned from my excursion renewed in body and spirit, and what happens? What do you think?" He ticked them off on the fingers of his left hand with the index finger of his right: "Madame Plourde has twins, Thomas Leblanc broke his left leg, Paul Bourgeois his right, young Luc Belliveau cut his wrist with an oyster-knife and the curé's arthritis has become worse. *Bon Dieu!* Why was I ever a doctor?"

"Because you love being a doctor."

Marc's smile was flashing and wholesome. "You have said it. But sometimes I feel as if I could write poetry or romances. Seeing you sitting there on Feu Follet and the light on your hair and in your eyes, I rise far, far above broken limbs and bruises and hardening arteries — yes, and even twins. Come! Leave Feu Follet at the White Roe and ride with me to Cormier's Cove. I shall be only a moment — just long enough to see if old Julie has died yet. She has been dying for ten years. Do come, Armande. It is so long since I have seen you."

"A few weeks only. But I shall go with you, Marc. Wait for me at the inn."

At the White Roe, Feu Follet was handed over to the proud care of Gil d'Entremont and Armande got into the car beside Marc.

"The last time you rode with me," he said, as they rolled away, "was that awful night when you came to fetch me on an errand of mercy. You recall?"

"I do not easily forget. In fact, I have been reminded of it afresh, for is not this John Gower still in St. Bruno?"

"Yes." Marc nodded. "Yes, he seems to like it here. A most unusual fellow. Interesting, too, but very puz-

THE WITCH AND THE PEASANT

zling. I do not know what to make of him. He — what shall I say — he seems to have lost whatever set of values he had — lost them in that storm — and found a new set. He lives at the White Roe and philosophizes with Isaac Proux or any of the other available wiseacres and insists that this is the place he has been looking for all his life."

"Today he works for Alyre Sormany at building-dikes."

"*Misère!* That, if anything, should cure him of his love for St. Bruno. Nothing like blisters on the hands and a crick in the back to fix one's values. There's no nonsense about those things."

"He seemed to like the work."

"You talked with him?"

"Yes. For a moment. He stopped. I — "

Marc looked at her out of the corner of his eye. "He piques you, Armande?"

"Oh, no, I think not that. It's just as you say. He is such a puzzle. Last night he said — " She caught herself up, a slow flush mounted to her cheek. Well, what if she had seen him last night? It was nothing to

FOG OVER FUNDY

Marc. "He walked along the road with me from the church where I had been playing. He said he felt like one who had been catapulted from another planet."

"Well," said Marc dryly. "It is very interesting indeed. He told you he was going to stay in St. Bruno?"

"Yes. He said he would be a cobbler or the like. Now he has found work on the dikes. He is not ambitious."

"No?" Marc's nostrils widened. "No? I wonder."

"What do you mean? You begin to speak in riddles too."

"Riddles, dear Armande, such as I propound or such as M'sieur John Gower might propound, are never riddles to a woman. Now are they? Tell me."

"You are too astute, Marc. You leave me defenseless."

"I am sorry. Come, we will talk no more about that. We come now to the Cove and to the residence of Madame Julie Thibodeau. You will wait?"

"I will come with you."

"She is very old. Her mind is apt to wander," whispered Marc as they walked up the path through the faded garden to the door of the white cottage on the

THE WITCH AND THE PEASANT

cliff's edge overlooking the Cove.

The ancient dame sat in a big wooden rocker in the living-room. There were neat hooked rugs on the hard-scrubbed floorboards, photographs and a picture of the Virgin on the walls; geraniums flaunted their pretty blooms on the window-sill.

"How do you find yourself today, Madame Thibodeau?" said Marc. "I see you still disobey me and will not stay in bed. That is a good sign."

"I am very well indeed," mumbled the old lady, peering up at Armande over her glasses. " Very well — Ah — ! " She bobbed her head vigorously until her cap all but tumbled off, sitting rakishly on one ear. "It is the young Ma'm'selle de Vysart."

"*Oui*, madame." Armande bowed and smiled, and took the old one's bone-dry fingers in her soft warm hand.

"You are not a witch then? They say you are a witch."

Armande shook her head, smiled at Marc with unparted lips.

"You are with the doctor. Not in love with the doctor, no? de Vysarts don't marry peasants — not even doctors."

Marc flushed crimson. Armande said nothing, for there was nothing to say. She wished she had not come here. The brightness was gone from the day. Folly. An old dame's mouthings. "Adieu, madame," she said. "I'll wait for you outside, Marc."

She was smoking a cigarette at the gate when Marc came out of the cottage. He smiled at her bravely. For answer she took his hand and pressed it hard. His eyes filled momentarily; then he laughed. "You are a witch, Armande. I came out of that place hating everything and old women in particular; now it does not seem to matter."

"Nothing matters, Marc, except what is true and what is good. And you are both, Marc, and you matter very much to me."

"And any man," he said, "should be content with that."

"You can, Marc."

"I have to be," he said, with no bitterness.

CHAPTER VI

THE FIRST SNOW

THE big car, spattered and streaked with the red-brown mud of the marshes, and filmed gray with dust, was parked in front of Beausejour when Armande returned from the ride that had witnessed Marc's discomfiture and her own embarrassment. She noted the bits of cord still dangling from the spokes of the spare wheel in the fender-well, to which Ulric was in the habit of lashing the soft and ruined carcass of some splendid moose or gentle-eyed deer that had fallen prey to his marksmanship. And she thought it unutterably cruel and unjust that one who did so little to add to life should be so free to rob the harmless forest-dwellers of their own happy existence.

Ulric, immense in brown corduroys and high-laced boots, came out of the house and hailed her cheerfully.

FOG OVER FUNDY

"A great trip," he announced. "And a splendid bag. Between the general and me, three moose, two deer and any number of woodcock. I tell you it was a great fortnight. The woods around the South Branch up there are alive with hunters. Well, how have you been? What have you been doing?"

"Going over the farm, seeing the dry-rot and desolation." Armande did not look at him. She stroked Feu Follet's glossy neck and laid her cheek against the satin smoothness of her coat. "Tumbledown barns and mice-ridden granaries, ruined fields and falling fences."

All the joy went out of Ulric's pale eyes. So that was it! Snooping around. Finding fault with his administration. Sticking her nose in where it had no business to be. He had been so sure she'd forget all that nonsense that he had quite ceased to think about it himself. "Well," he said slowly, "we'll see what can be done, though it is not only senseless but — but really impossible to spend money on improvements now. Stocks and shares, you know, have dwindled away to nothing, the rewards of farming are ridiculously small. All one can do is mark time and hope for an upswing."

THE FIRST SNOW

"Poultry and bacon-hogs," continued Armande imperturbably, looking at Feu Follet, who rolled an appreciative eye at her. "The Old Country market was never better. Lots of money to be made there — turkeys, chickens, eggs and the like — "

"You talk like some farmer's wench," said Ulric angrily. "Why should you give a curse about such things as a lot of silly hens and grunting swine?"

"They built this place, Ulric. They made life possible for you and me. You talk as if the world, our world, the world of our family ended with you and me."

"With me, yes; with you, seemingly."

"I think not." She flushed angrily and led Feu Follet towards the stables. "Life goes on, Ulric. You may have a surprise one of these days."

"What do you mean?" bawled Ulric, but she did not answer him nor even look back. She was thinking of that village girl, Suzanne Delagarde and her son. Queer about them. Yet everything seemed to be all right. There had been no talk in a community that had no rival in the country at being quick to find matter for gossip. The boy's father, she recalled, had been

FOG OVER FUNDY

drowned, just about the time the little fellow must have started on his way. She wrinkled her brow, trying to think, to remember about Leon. Though popular with women and happy in their companionship, he had never been a philanderer nor yet a rake. He had been, she knew, too strong, too much a man for any cheap seduction or any trifling with another's wife. Yet there had been something terribly real in Suzanne's grieving, and in young Paul Emil's eyes too was that which had always, without her knowing it, awakened a warm and quick response from Armande. A puzzle, all of it. She would have gone to Suzanne, questioned her, but that she feared the accusation of prying and had seen, too, in the way Suzanne turned from her, in Suzanne's dark sullenness, a hostility that she knew only too well, the hostility of the peasant, which only something cataclysmic can budge.

Ulric said, over the noonday venison: "I have heard from Roger, about Leon. They are still looking for the man Dumont, but he seems to have vanished into thin air. There is no question in the minds of the police that he is the guilty one."

THE FIRST SNOW

"His running away would seem to indicate that. Well, perhaps he carries his punishment with him, in his heart."

"Little chance. You do not know much, Armande, if you think a man who could do a thing like that would feel much remorse."

"But he might have done it in anger. No doubt he did. And that girl over whom they quarrelled — how must she feel?"

"Women bear such things lightly," said Ulric with his mouth full. "It makes them feel important that a man should kill or be killed for them."

Armande shook her head. "I cannot understand such a thing, Ulric."

"Perhaps if men fought over you, it would become clear to you. Not much likelihood of that, since you persist in burying yourself here in St. Bruno. I don't see why you haven't gone away. It is the first Autumn you have missed a visit to Montreal or New York or some place where there is a bit of life."

"I told you why I was staying home."

"We won't talk about it," muttered Ulric sullenly.

FOG OVER FUNDY

"Not now, perhaps. But soon, Ulric — soon."

"Confound it! If you — " He stopped, clamped his lips tight. Armande shrugged. Presently, she finished her light meal, excused herself and left the table. She went, with Sirdar trotting beside her, to her room. The afternoon promised to be bleak and dismal. There was snow in the north wind that whistled boisterously about the tower. Snow would be good, she thought. It would cover with its pure white spread the ugly brown of the marshes, the dull black of the hills.

She put a match to the dry cedar chips under the logs of rock-maple in the great stone hearth and sat down with Sirdar on the black bearskin-rug to watch the flames lick upward. She loved the security, the solitude of her room. It was so very much her own — the pictures and little trophies of her days at school and college, souvenirs of strange cities and far-off lands that seemed to bring the great world outside into the quiet room in this lonely house on the edge of the Tantramar, and to give her a deeper appreciation of how tranquil life could be here and how good and happy.

The joy of life flowed in her today like a warm rich

THE FIRST SNOW

stream. The grim gray sky meant nothing, nor the faded land nor the blue smoke blowing down from the chimney past her window, nor the threat of winter in the wind. For it was warm by the fire and the hissing sound of the flames, their deep-voiced rumble in the wide flue, were good sounds, loved and familiar. She thought of the long hours ahead that she would spend by her fire, growing old by the flames that are ever young. Long hours rich with beauty. And not always alone. No, there would be good friends, true hearts, and —

"There is a moon tonight." The half-shy, halting invitation of those words, the secret hope they voiced, haunted her. It was as if he wanted to share in the beauty of the magic hours that she had ever been able to steal from life. As if he sought to be admitted to the mystic kinship she had with sea and sky and the night. And he was backward, afraid, as if, perhaps, he thought himself unworthy of the high rapture she knew.

"I will not go tonight," she decided, looking sombrely at the driving clouds, at the few tattered leaves on the vines. "Anyway, there will be no moon tonight,

FOG OVER FUNDY

and he, I fancy, will hug the fireside in the White Roe."

Even as she watched, the snow began to fall — the first snow, gossamer-light and feathery, in scattered flakes. It tapped softly against the windowpane, it mottled the lawn with little spots of white, melting at first, as if the earth resisted them, then gradually taking hold, spreading a lovely mantle over the corpse of the summer, while the black north wind sang its requiem. And as she watched it, with emotions sad and joyful, she thought of the many others who gazed upon it from their windows; how the children's bright eyes sparkled brighter at thought of sleds and skates and snowmen and forts for mimic warfare; how the farmer, his cellar and larder well stocked, his dooryard stacked with wood and his house banked warmly with earth, felt in his heart the contentment that comes with security, with work well done and loved ones well protected; of the lonely wayfarer, the tramper of the moors, whose bed was a bit of straw in some drafty barn or a burrow in a stack or merely the frozen shelter of a hedge.

Until long after the dark had fallen the snow sifted

THE FIRST SNOW

lightly down; then the moonrays rifted the clouds, bursting them asunder, leaving jagged edges of smoky gray and shining brightly down on the new snow, making it jewel and shimmer as when a spotlight is turned upon the white sequined satin of some great diva's robe.

" There is a moon tonight."

Ulric, still weary from his weeks in the woods, had gone to bed. Armande slipped out of the silent house into that strange new world of silver and dazzling white. The powdery snow muffled the sound of her footsteps. It was soft and good to walk upon. In the churchyard it was unmarked by any footprints and she was glad of that, for she liked to play alone. It was easier to express what was in her heart when there were none to hear. She did not mind the drafty chill of the choir-loft; she loved the resonance of the rich organ tones that seemed to shed some electric warmth all about her.

Somehow, tonight, she could not lose herself in her playing, in the singing throb of the great instrument that answered like a living thing the skilled touch of her fingers. But she did not feel his eyes upon her tonight. She did not sense his presence. It did not matter; yet

FOG OVER FUNDY

she felt a loneliness, a sensation of being let-down, as she closed the organ and threaded her way among the empty benches. There was that in her heart, an unrest, a discontent, that this night, for the first time, the music had failed to satisfy. It had nothing to do with this man, she told herself; it could not concern him —

The quick leap of her heart when she saw him standing in the vestibule at the foot of the choir steps gave the lie to all that. She was glad; more than glad. She felt absurdly happy and contented to see his dark eyes gazing up at her, marking her descent. She was too honest to feign surprise, to pretend that she had not looked for his presence.

"So you saw the moon!" she said, pausing on the bottom step in a shaft of blue-silver light.

He came to her; his eyes were almost on a level with hers. "I prayed for the moon," he said. "I prayed for it as, I think, I never before prayed for anything. And my prayers were heard. I stayed here. I thought if I came up you might not like it; you might stop playing. I stayed here to listen. Do you know, your music does something to a man. It seems to bring things to life in

THE FIRST SNOW

a man's heart. It lifts him up high and makes life a wondrous thing."

"It does that to you — my music!"

"Your music — and you. I cannot say it. I should not try —"

Again that urge, that madness, pushed her on to say what all reason, all good-sense — those things so beloved of Ulric — forbade her saying — "Try," she whispered.

"You — you seem to possess me, to be like a spell upon me. I can think only of you — your eyes, your hair that is like a mystic light, the beauty that is all about you. And you humble me, so that I want to go on my knees and worship you."

"No. You must not feel like that about me. Why should you? I — well, I am just Armande —"

"I adore you," he said earnestly. "I know that all my life will be too short a time to give to that adoration."

"You do me great honor, m'sieur. You make me proud; for you, yourself, are strong and good."

"I?" He shook his head and looked at her gravely.

FOG OVER FUNDY

"You think that?" His tone was eager. "You believe I am strong and good?"

"I believe," she said simply. His arms came up and encircled her, gently, almost reverently and strained her to him for a swift, breathless moment in which his lips rested hungrily on her hair, on her cheek, on the softness of her mouth; a moment in which she felt all the latent force of her spirit rise up to meet his ardour, to match it, to merge with it. Then, slowly, he released her and stood gazing up at her as one in a dream who fears awaking.

"God," he whispered. "You are lovely. You are lovely beyond words! You bring me happiness so great that I never could have believed in it!"

She did not speak, but her eyes did not waver from his. They stood there for long moments gazing at each other. He touched her hand. "Come, Armande." They walked out of the church, down the white path among the graves and up the road to Beausejour. That moment of beauty still lingered with them; they walked in a mist of happiness that shut out all the world beyond and surrounded them alone. It did not occur to

THE FIRST SNOW

her that she knew nothing of this man; that he was a mystery and that he said nothing to dispel that mystery. Cobbler, carpenter, fisherman, builder of dikes — it did not matter. What would Ulric say? And Roger? And Marc? And the Tantramar folk? It did not matter. Nothing mattered, save that they walked together and did not need to speak, whose hearts were in closest communion. Thus they came to the gates of Beausejour. At the end of the white sweep of driveway, between the dark rows of cedars, the walls rose gray and forbidding, the moonlight glinting on the windows.

She turned to him, lifted her face to his kiss. " It is madness, no doubt," she whispered, clinging to him. " But I love it."

" Madness? " He released her suddenly. " Why do you say that? It is the loveliest thing in the world. And you — I know you can take it without question, without reservation. You must take it so, for I — " He did not go on.

" I can take it so."

" If I were to die now," he said. " I would be happy, for I have known this thing. I have known you. Living, all my days will be bright and my nights full of beauty."

"You are no seafarer, John Gower, A. B."

"No," he said slowly. "No, I think not. I — I am just a man who loves you, my dear. Inadequate, is it not?"

"Strangely, strangely adequate," said Armande.

"I know!" he said triumphantly. "You are one among many, Armande — one in all the world perhaps. You do not question what I am —"

"I know."

"Or where I came from."

"I do not care."

"Or what I shall do."

"You will love me. La-la!" She touched his lips with her fingers. "Surely we two are creatures of the moon. Quite, quite mad the world would call us. One old lady asked me only this day if I were not a witch. But she said I was not."

"A witch — yes, they say you are, the people. 'The Moon Witch,' they call you. And thinking of you, looking at you, I can see how they can believe there is something supernatural about you. But you are warm in my

THE FIRST SNOW

arms and your kiss does not bring Death."

She shivered. " Do not say that! "

" But why? "

" You bring shivers along my spine. To you, only to you, I have given my kiss. It cannot bring to you anything that is not good and right. Death — what an ugly thought! "

" I should not have said it. Forgive me. And forget about it."

She touched his hand. He caught her fingers and pressed them to his lips. " Good night," he said. " You have been good to me. You have been an angel of light. I love you — love you, do you hear! "

" I cannot hear too often. This love — it is a strange thing. It is something that dwarfs all other considerations, makes little of time and place and circumstances. Here I have lived all my life and have not found it, and, presto, you come out of the sea and the storm and are presented to me on the porch of the White Roe and you bring love to me and all the world is different." She spread her arms wide, lifted her face to the sky. " The night is brighter, the land more fair to see, tomorrow

FOG OVER FUNDY

will be golden. But, m'sieur — " Her arms dropped to her sides and she tilted her head gravely. She wanted to say, " There was a look of hell in your eyes that night and in your delirium you called another name than mine — Candace." She did not say it. She did not want to spoil this hour, to take away one little bit from her happiness. Life, for him, for her, had begun tonight and whatever had gone before did not concern her. Sometime he would speak of it, no doubt; she would know sometime what his life had been before he came to her. Just now it was her love of him that mattered, that ousted all other thoughts from her mind.

" Goodnight," she whispered. " Soon we shall meet again."

" Soon," he echoed, and stood watching her until she passed under the deep shadow of the portico.

L'Etranger — the Stranger, they called him in St. Bruno; and for a time made little of his presence in their midst. It had happened often before along the Fundy Coast, that men cast up by the sea had settled in the place where they touched the blessed land. There

THE FIRST SNOW

were stories of strange castaways who had never spoken nor vouchsafed any information of who they were or whence they had come; there was one they called Portagee William, a dark man who had lived in the hull of an old barge cast-up by the tide on the sand-flats. And Portagee William, it was rumored, had been a duke, or at least a count in the land he hailed from.

So, to the simple folk of St. Bruno, John Gower was just another one of the sea's many riddles. The council of ancients that, like druids, encircled the fire in the White Roe's parlor, did their best with him, so did Isaac Proux; but, as they had very little English and l'Etranger had less French, they did not get very far. It was conceded that he must be a poor man and that he stayed in St. Bruno to work merely in order to make money sufficient to take him back to the States.

But it was queer, as Isaac said, that he should tramp the marshes in the dead of night. And it was certain that he had not the ways of a seafaring man nor did his hands look as if they'd seen much of ropes or tiller-spokes. Then, too, there were the books that had been left at the White Roe by a queer Englishman who used

FOG OVER FUNDY

to paint and write poetry — books of verse and essays and novels by Russians with long, outlandish names. Isaac had thrown them all into the attic when the curé, glancing over them, said that some were written by the devil with a pen dipped in corruption. But John Gower had pounced upon them with a gleam of delight in his eyes and often Isaac or Elodie heard him reading aloud as he paced up and down his room.

Perhaps it would not have taken the villagers long to become used to him, and, while not accepting him in their fellowship — it took three generations for that — at least to leave him to his own devices, had it not been for Isaac Proux's grandmother, the good soul dead these sixty years but commemorated always by a high mass of requiem upon the day following Martinmas. The first snow had fallen on Martinmas and it was on St. Martin's night that Armande de Vysart's silken hair had brushed John Gower's cheek and her lips first touched his. And from the side door of the church-tower their footprints, alone in the virgin snow, greeted the eyes of Isaac and Elodie and some score more of the Proux and Gastonguay families when in the frosty

THE FIRST SNOW

morning they trudged through the churchyard on their way to mass.

Their eyes were sharp. No one used that door except Phelonèse Girard, the regular organist, and Armande de Vysart. Clearly these were not the footprints of Phelonèse, who had a club-foot and carried a cane and walked like a rocking-chair. These prints, one set of them, showed small and shapely, the others large and studded as if made by the boots of a labourer. Eyes looked into eyes with question and startled wonder. "Those," whispered Elodie to Anna Gaudet, her cousin, "look like the prints of the new boots bought by l'Etranger a day or so ago. I noted the pattern of them in the inn-yard this morning."

"And the others are hers — those of the Moon Witch — She who pulled him from the sea!"

"But that they should meet together by night in the House of God! It is sinful, just as it is sinful for her to play her crazy music in the night when all good people are warm in their beds and only werewolves and evil spirits walk the earth. Perhaps this man is the devil, come for a rendezvous with her. And where better could

FOG OVER FUNDY

the devil and a witch have rendezvous than in the church?"

The word went quickly around. There was much distraction during the mass and if Isaac's grandmother, who had been Claudette Gastonguay, stood much in need of the yearly prayers to shorten her stay in purgatory, it is to be feared that very few days were lopped off her sentence. Here was something that gripped their simple fancies — something occult and fascinating, this stranger from the sea and the Moon Witch. Spells and charms and broomstick rides over the roofs of the cottages, over the tall church-spire. Ah, what now had come to St. Bruno, what was afoot that these two should meet secretly by night in the hallowed ground?

Nothing good. It could be nothing good. There was a great deal of excitement and head-shaking and muttered conversation as Isaac and his kinsmen left the church with many a speculative look at the little prints of Armande's shoes and the patterned impress of l'Etranger's shoe-packs in the snow.

"Night before last," said Pamphile Gastonguay, "was the full o' the moon — a night clear and bright

THE FIRST SNOW

as silver and a night on which, I tell you, my friends, you could almost see many ghostly things, let alone fancy them. I had been playing cards quite late at Marcel Gaudet's and I did not loiter on my homeward way. As I passed the church I heard her playing — the Moon Witch — such music as, I swear, no mortal hand could get out of the church organ. Phelonèse Girard's playing sounds like noises from a tin can compared with what that one played. Music not of earth, *mes amis*. I crossed myself and hurried faster. I wouldn't enter the church at dead of night, none of us would; and tell me the young girl who would have courage to sit there in the darkness and play music."

" I'll wager," muttered Hormidas Breau, the cobbler, " that the disembodied spirits misted up out of the grave and joined hands and danced about the tomb-stones. I tell you the curé should know of this and the church be closed to her. No good can come of it. And l'Etranger — it may be that he is the Evil One himself whom she has summoned upon the earth. Look you, since his coming, her own brother has gone — murdered. Who can tell what else may happen. She could put a spell on

FOG OVER FUNDY

any one of us. Look! Regard! But do not let her see that one notices too closely."

The cobbler and his companions and the others of the congregation following them along the village street, ceased talking and looked slyly from eye-corners at the tall figure of Armande de Vysart, at the little boy, so rosy-cheeked and angelic, who walked beside her. She had her gloved hand on his shoulder and he was smiling up at her. Not one there, among those furtive watchers but saw the startling likeness between them, the same proud beauty about them both — and marvelled at it.

Ignorant of their dark thoughts, of all their talk of ghosts and spells, Armande smiled at the villagers and sensed no hostility in their greetings. Like all the Tantramar folk she was an early riser and would start no day without an excursion into the open air. She wore a tailored suit of reddish brown homespun, a careless black felt hat, fawn stockings and buckled clogs adapted to the snow and mud of the marshes. She carried a light maple-stick, the hound Sirdar shambled

THE FIRST SNOW

along behind her and the little dancing form of Paul Emil Delagarde.

"The Moon Witch has put a spell on the young Delagarde, for sure," muttered the cobbler. " Even, he begins to look like her. A changeling, no doubt; likely Gregoire Delagarde's son went down into the sea with him and this one was given to Suzanne in his stead. She will win him away from the mother. See how he smiles up at her! As if she owned him! "

It was true enough. The boy's great blue eyes gazed adoringly up into the gentle, lovely face bent above him. He loved the companionable feel of her hand on his shoulder, the roughness of her sleeve when it brushed his cheek. His own mother was kind and good, though there were times when she was very silent and times when she was angry with him for no reason at all. Too, she had scolded him the day of Leon de Vysart's funeral, when he had smiled and waved at Armande. She had said, his mother; " What have you to do with that one! We are only poor folk, we have nothing in common with her. She wouldn't look at a peasant's brat except it had a pretty face like yours. Sometimes — sometimes

FOG OVER FUNDY

I hate your pretty face, Paul Emil, and wish you were dark-skinned and coarse-featured and shrill-voiced like the other children."

And Paul Emil had looked at her wonderingly; not understanding at all what she meant, still stoutly loyal to the beautiful lady whose eyes filled with gladness every time she saw him, who smelt of strange fragrant perfume, of what he knew was lavender from having seen and sniffed it in the store of Ephraim Melanson, the apothecary. Of the difference between prince and peasant he was not conscious. It was a mystery to him that his mother should frown, that her lips should tighten and her eyes turn away when Armande de Vysart passed them.

He saw that very phenomenon now, in front of the post-office. Suzanne Delagarde with a few letters and a bright colored catalogue came out of the post-office as Armande and Paul Emil arrived in front of it. The devout worshippers from the black mass still straggled along the far side of the street, and they too saw Suzanne's pale brow grow dark, saw her lips narrow and her eyes look sullenly at the girl with her son. They

THE FIRST SNOW

could not tell what she said, but they could readily guess. Paul Emil, reluctantly but with unquestioning obedience, left the shelter of Armande's side and went to his mother. And Suzanne did not speak another word nor again glance at Armande, but took her boy by the hand and walked quickly down the street.

"Suzanne is wise," said Hormidas. "She does well to keep her young one away from the de Vysart, lest he be changed into a black dog or a raven and spirited away."

Armande, feeling defeat and helplessness, hurried quickly into the post-office and got her mail. She had mastered with a mighty effort the wild pulsing anger that tore like flame through her body when Suzanne Delagarde called the little boy away from her. She had looked at Suzanne and smiled and said, "Why? Do you think he is not well with me?" And the woman had said nothing, merely taken the little fellow and gone away. As well, Armande knew, try to turn the river from its course or move the church-steeple a league, as seek to penetrate the armor of hostility that Suzanne wore. The woman was poor, having only the

FOG OVER FUNDY

little cottage Gregoire had left her, down by the shore; and a few dollars of income that she made by sewing. Poor, but boundlessly wealthy in pride, in her peasant stubbornness. With such as she, a secret to keep, and a yoke of oxen could not drag it from her; a person to hate and only a first-class miracle could temper it into tolerance.

"And she looks," mused Armande, "as though she might not have any too much to eat at times. She would go without, I know, to give it to him — so would I."

She walked through the village in the direction of Beausejour, slowly, opening her mail as she went along. There were letters for her and Ulric from Roger Lavergne. She opened hers and read the graceful, flowing script. It was the old plea all over again —

Come! The first snow has fallen and the slopes of Mount Royal are white with it and the dome of the basilica and the towers of Notre Dame are lovely under the moon. You would be so happy here, Armande. All the shops are preparing for Christmas, and such furs and silks and jewels you never saw.

THE FIRST SNOW

How I should love to go again with you up the Mount for a ride on the mad toboggan or to the Seigneurie Club to sit by the roaring fire and read beauty in your eyes. Armande! Armande! I come back to it, as I must, as I always shall. Come to me. Leave your ice-bound, misty marshes and your gray sea, and come. I love you.

So easy to do. Furs and silks and jewels; the dim-lit lobbies of great hotels with the world at play passing in and out; the murmurous drawing-rooms of palaces of wealth, the rapier flash of wit, the sparkle of wine; Roger, a gallant knight, forever at her side, his wealth, his title an open sesame to the strongest barred portals in the land. Laughter and warmth and gay companions, life all a colored dream, with no awaking. How bitter was the marsh-wind this morning; how iron-hard the ruts in the frozen road; how blackish brown and turgid the river flowing to the sea through the dead white plain of the marshes. And the sky ice-cold, blue and clear, and frost covering the cottage windows along her road.

FOG OVER FUNDY

Why stay here? Why not go to Montreal, if only for a visit? Why worry about Ulric and Beausejour — a pile of rocks, a lot of fruitless fields. She was young and life all before her; why sacrifice herself for a formless dream, an unvoiced hope? Why? To linger here — and now she knew the why of her lingering; what more than pride of birth or possession — held her here. Something in a man's eyes, in his voice, his touch. Casually to dismiss the things most dear to women, security, peace, sane romance — for a love unknown, unguessed-at, for a kiss in silver moonlight and black velvet shadow, for warm breath in her hair, for strong arms about her —

For a love whose future was beyond the wildest conjecture, an unknown land, an uncharted sea. Nothing to guide her — only faith. But she was strong in faith, stronger still in her loyalties, no matter how sudden their springing up, how strange or seemingly ignoble their object. All the world, be it gray and black sea and sky and icy wind and frozen ground — was glad today. There was a song in her heart and she loved the sting of the wind, the nip of frost, the ring of hard heels on

THE FIRST SNOW

the iron ground, the way the white shell-ice in the puddles cracked under the ferrule of her stick, the way the big Afghan sniffed the zesty wind, eyes sparkling, thick coat crisp with winter.

> I send you some papers with accounts of the tragedy. You may not wish to read them. I thought you might, now that some little time has passed; enough to soothe the first sharp pain. They have had no success in their search for Dumont. Fear and guilt, it is obvious, are the things that drive him. Why else should a man throw up wealth and ease and skulk under cover like a jackal. A cowardly murderer, it is obvious.
>
> R.

The tragedy, the way this man had run off, the search for him, all seemed unreal and unimportant to her now. People of another world, things that had no relation to her. Best, as swiftly as possible to forget them. The life of Broadway, of the hot spots, of gay spending, of eternal dancing on the brink of ruin, the life at which Leon had taken his fling was not the life of the marsh-

FOG OVER FUNDY

lands. The two had nothing in common save humanity. To read of this thing, then, she thought, would be like reading some story, to picture it like watching some play. The Leon in it would not be the Leon she had known.

Idly she opened the rolled up journals and glanced over them. There were pictures — photographs of Leon de Vysart, of Iris Wayland, of Sunset Lodge, a lovely log chalet among the trees on the shore of a mountain lake; a picture of Michael Dumont — " Fugitive," it said beneath it —

" *Bon jour, comptesse!* " A hearty voice hailed her. Marc Duclos' voice. Hastily she folded the newspaper and tucked it under her arm. She smiled at him. " *Salut, M'sieur le docteur!* " Marc doffed his cap. He fell in step beside her.

" *Ecoute donc,* Armande." He was very earnest. He frowned. He pursed his lips. She had to step lively to keep up with his nervous, energetic striding. " Signor Marconi is a fool compared with some of these Prouxs and Gastonguays and the like."

" What now, Marc? " She was only half listening to

THE FIRST SNOW

him. The bloomy color had ebbed from her cheeks, leaving them white and wan.

"I mean to say," continued Marc, "that their diffusion of news is faster and more thorough than the good Guglielmo's could ever hope to be. And they can make news if there is none. They have it over him there too."

"How does this concern me?"

"I was at Antoine Proux's house early — baby with the croup. The girl Philomèle returned from the mass for the old Gastonguay. She did not know I was in the bedroom. She said —

"Yes, Marc. What is it?"

"They saw footprints in the churchyard snow," said Marc uneasily. "They say you were there at night with this stranger who stays at the White Roe."

"It is true. What of it?"

"Armande! You know these people. These — well, maybe I know them better than you, being one of them."

"It was but a chance meeting," said Armande. "What can they make of that?"

"You do not then know them. 'Moon Witch,' they

FOG OVER FUNDY

call you. And they said — how unutterably insane and incredible in this country, in this day! — that this poor fellow is the Evil One, come up out of the sea."

"At that, they may be right, Marc," she said. "How cold and grim it is this morning!"

"I do not mind it."

It came to her when he spoke that a few moments ago she had not minded it either.

CHAPTER VII

PAUL EMIL

"WHAT folly is this!" Big Ulric, chin out-thrust, feet planted wide apart on the white bear-rug before the living-room fire, glared at Armande. Five nights now since she had played in St. Bruno's Church, five nights since she had seen John Gower. The bright moon was waning. It would be late, late tonight before its wasting sphere would loom up over the eastern hills. Dusk now, with only the flickering light of the fire casting a gigantic shadow of Ulric on the dim walls of the room; twilight gray and lonely settling over the white of the marshes; over the dark of the river, over the restless sea.

"Of what do you speak?" She had been back from a long ride on Feu Follet only time enough to bathe, to change from the worn riding-habit to a dress of bright

FOG OVER FUNDY

blue wool that made her very young and small and girlish. The blue eyes that looked into Ulric's, so much paler, so much less bright, were guileless and questioning. Ulric was drinking again. He had started a few days after his return from the hunt. He would go on drinking, she knew; he said there was nothing else to occupy him — nothing else, while the place went to rack and ruin all about him.

"Folly!" he repeated. "This insane conduct of yours. It wasn't bad enough to act like a wild thing, to roam wide and free all over the Tantramar in storms and weather not fit for a — a dog to be out in. No! You must now have yourself and your name linked up with some worthless tramp, some fellow you picked up out of the mud, when it would have been a lot better to have let him die. Even so, having done that, what more? What else should you have to do with him?"

"What else? Why, he is a man — a human being like the rest of us. He seemed — even different from the rest."

"Was that why you met him in the middle of the night — and at the church, above all places?" Ulric sneered. " A pretty mess indeed! "

" I see nothing to it. And why not at the church as well as any other place? There was no harm in our meeting — " Her eyes were soft, dreamy — " no harm whatever, Ulric; and those who could read anything wrong into it are only to be pitied. You would not have me pity you? "

" Pity me! I do not need your pity, ma'moiselle! It is you, talked about, stared at, disliked even, who stand in need of pity."

" I need it no more than you. And surely you do not heed the talk of people you always looked down upon as peasants."

" Yes! That is it! Just because they are peasants we owe to them the responsibility of keeping in our places and keeping them in theirs."

" I have harmed none of them. You talk foolishly, Ulric." She sighed wearily, put her hands behind her head and leant back against the settle. " I can know only my own way; it is to be supposed, pray God, that I know that way better than any other could know it; so I must go that way. Wrong, evil, sinful, worse — I must go it! "

"What sort of talk is this to come from you! Surely there is nothing — *Seigneur!* You do not sit there brazenly and tell me that there is anything between this wretched fellow and you! "

"One calls it love, Ulric," she murmured softly, watching the flames with sleepy-lidded eyes. "Love, you know. It has built empires and destroyed them, made kings and unmade them. It is the living thread that runs all through life, through the history of the world. It is a strange and wondrous thing. Once you know it, there seems to be nothing else in life for you."

"Love! " Ulric's mouth sagged open. "Love for this — ! You are joking. This is some more of your foolery. Why — how could you be in love with the man? "

"Ah, that is one of the things about love, my brother. The questions that you can apply to the ordinary things of life, you cannot apply at all successfully to love. It defies question and analysis. You say, 'Why' and 'How.' I answer, 'I do not know why or how. It is; that

PAUL EMIL

is all I know. A great puzzle, Ulric."

"You act like a madwoman, Armande, I swear. No wonder these ignorant peasants call you a witch —"

"Yes," she murmured, "a witch. Do you know, Ulric, I should like very much to be a witch. To have great power, but only over evil. I should be a kind witch, tempering evil, eradicating it, turning it into good. And —" Deftly she switched the talk — "I should begin at Beausejour. I would turn all the brandy into water, I would fix the house, put new carpets on the floors, new paper on the walls, new furniture here and there in the rooms. In the stables I would, with a wave of my magic wand, put some good horses and in the carriage shed, wagons; these I would make out of pumpkins and mice after the manner of that good witch, the fairy godmother in Cinderella. You recall Cinderella, Ulric?"

"I will not talk to you." He was strangely unperturbed. "I have done with you, with it all."

"Not by any means." She sat up suddenly, looking fiercely at him. "You are the head of this house. How can you say you are done with it all! You have a great task, a man's task, ahead of you."

"Have I! Suppose you do it with some of your magic. Put a few spells on the place. Summon up some sacks of gold pieces."

"We have money — my money — Leon's — "

"Yes, yes, of course."

"But you were to render an account of it. Long ago, you were to do that. And you have delayed, put it off, purposely, I think. I am entitled to know. I must know. If you will do nothing for Beausejour, then I must do it myself and you must furnish me the means to do it with."

"We shall see." Ulric licked his loose lips. "It is a pity — all a terrible pity." He adopted an injured tone, looked at her almost wistfully with his bleary, bloodshot eyes.

"What is a pity?" It was hard to be patient with him. She knew his injured tone, his suffering look. "The ruin all about us?"

"No. No; I mean that you and Roger — "

"Never."

"Well, that is why I say it is all a pity. You could

PAUL EMIL

then do what you wished with the place. You could tear it down and build another, if you were so minded. But you wouldn't be; you wouldn't care at all about this old rookery and these miles of mud."

" Ulric — " Her voice was very gentle — " God pity you if you see in this house only an old rookery and in these broad fields only miles of mud — "

" But — "

" This is still a noble house. Its cornerstones are Love and Hope and Trust and Strength. Those are the keys on which it is built. No decay can ever touch them, time does nothing to them, for they are timeless. And these lands of ours — the very blood and life of our people are in the soil. You talk like that! How can you talk like that! "

" I — well, I do not see it the way you do," muttered Ulric. " Of course, hang it all, I have quite as much family pride as you. I am a de Vysart. I don't forget it. But I'm sensible. I know when I'm licked or when a thing isn't worth going on with. That's mature wisdom; what you have is a child's idealism, a lot of silly, romantic notions that will prove nothing but a heartbreak in the end."

"I shall have had them, at least."

"Small satisfaction, I tell you."

"*Bien!*" She stood up. The dinner gong sounded softly. "We shall never, I fear, see eye to eye, Ulric. It is a pity. I should like to go on with you, with one of my own flesh and blood, but failing that I shall go on alone."

"Yes," said Ulric. He smiled at the straight slim shoulders ahead of him. "You will."

Armande walked down the drive under the cold bright stars, their light reflecting dimly from the snow-covered lawns. The wind sighed deeply through the cedars and their spiral tips leaned close to each other, then away, then back again, like so many old women whispering dark secrets and gossip to each other. Ulric had spoken little during their dinner. Ulric, of late, had been more silent, more withdrawn than ever before. There were times when she caught him looking at her almost angrily as if he were blaming her for something,

PAUL EMIL

as if, mentally, he were levelling bitter accusations at her. Well, he had no cause to blame her. For years he had held full control over their fortunes. If things were wrong, it was his doing. Perhaps, she thought, he disliked her for disturbing his indolent existence, for trying to pull him up out of the slough of laziness and dissipation into which he had long ago descended. Whatever it was, she decided cheerfully, he would get over it; in time he would thank her. Happily, she visioned a new and better life at Beausejour, which would see her and Ulric working together to build up the fortunes of their house.

In the shadows of the tall gateway, a darker shadow lurked. She caught its movement as she passed through, out into the road. She heard him whisper, " Armande! " She stopped, the wind whipping her coat about her slender body, pulling at her pale tresses. He came close to her. He said, " It is so good to see you. I have been lost — more lost than ever, these several days. I've haunted the marshes and the church, by night, looking for you, seeing you in every shadow, hearing your voice in every whisper of the wind."

FOG OVER FUNDY

"You have missed me so much?"

"So much that I can realize better now what knowing you has meant to me. You have not been avoiding me?"

"I cannot say. Perhaps yes." She stood stiffly. He did not touch her nor try to take her in his arms.

"But why? Oh, I think I know. I have seen looks, heard words here and there. I begin to understand the language better. I had forgotten that St. Bruno is a small place, that people will talk —"

"Yes, I know that. People have talked. They saw our footprints in the snow by the church tower. They are quick to learn things, these people, and slow — you cannot think how slow — to forget them. And the absurd things they say — !"

"That you are a witch — the Moon Witch. I love the fancy. I love to think of you that way. It was under the moon that I saw your beauty, that I learned something of the wonder of you. You seem most lovely under the moon, like a strange flower that thrives most on that silver light."

"But of you, M'sieur John Gower, they say stranger

PAUL EMIL

still. They say that you are, if not the Black One himself, then some spirit high in his councils. They think that, out of the Abyss, you and I made rendezvous in the quiet church of this peaceful village. Probably they think we summon up flames from the frozen ground and sling a cauldron on a tripod and concoct strange hell-broths for our charms and spells. It is not so pleasant to be thought a witch when you don't have any witchly attributes."

"Except eyes that shine with a light from the skies and hair softer than any silk and — "

"You find me fair?" She looked at him with a wistfulness he could not see there in the pallid light of the stars. "Your own spell is as potent as mine — the spell of the lovely things you say to me. But I know, when you speak, that I am all woman, for I love to hear them and to believe them. For I do believe them. I want you to know." There was a deep intensity, an utter honesty in her voice. "I have listened and loved it and believed in all you have said, just as — just as I believe in a God who is good and kind."

FOG OVER FUNDY

"You can believe. I speak from my heart, from its deepest depths, Armande."

"You speak with the voice of angels, but — can not the Black One, if he wills it, speak with such a voice? But no; you are not he."

"Why do you speak of that? And you do not seem to jest — not entirely. You — you aren't given to these beliefs, to — "

She shook her head slowly. "No. No, I am not given to them. My creed is simple. Perhaps it is foolish. I believe in a thing and I continue to believe. If something that comes to you seems as if it could be sent only from heaven, then it should take a very great deal to make you turn around and believe that it came from hell."

"How strangely you talk, Armande!"

"Yes, perhaps strangely. And yet — Tell me: what do you do in the village now? They have not ostracized you?"

"No. Just the other way. They act queerly, but they are kind and most respectful. Maybe it is that they fear me and think it best to play safe. Anyway, I am working in the print-shop of old Trudel — sort of a

PAUL EMIL

printer's devil." He laughed. " Maybe they thought me best fitted for that job. My first day at it should have convinced Trudel otherwise. But I am learning; I get less ink on my hands."

" You will stay in St. Bruno then — really? "

" I will stay. One does not willingly go out of Paradise. And it is Paradise for me, because you are here."

" It is — because of me you stay here? "

" Is not that reason sufficient? "

" I believe. I will believe." Suddenly she was in his arms, trembling, her cheek pressed against his. He touched her lips, first lightly, with his; then lingeringly, with devastating passion, until she broke from him.

" What is it, Armande? What has disturbed you so? "

" Nothing. Oh, nothing. Go now! Go quickly! "

" But when — ? "

" When? I do not know. But soon. It will be soon." She turned and ran, stumbling, up the drive. Frowning, a dazed, wondering look in his eyes, he watched her until she was only a sound, the scuffling of heels on the bare spots of the gravel. " God help me," he muttered. " Do I do wrong here? What has come over her? It

FOG OVER FUNDY

must be this silly talk of devils and witches. She speaks as if she believed in it. But is there about me anything — " He shook his head savagely. " No. No. I won't give this up, won't even risk giving it up. I love her. That's all I know." He spoke wildly as he trudged away. " That's all I want to know. Isn't that enough for any man to know. I love her and she loves me and she believes in me. Good and strong — she told me I was good and strong. So I must be. She would know. Those eyes of hers can look into one's soul and see if it is dark or light." He gazed out at the murmurous blackness where the sea was, rushing, racing and tumbling against the great sea-walls. " Out there," he said. " That's a rare place to hide a thing. You never could find a thing that was lost in the sea. And if you don't know what it is you lost, why try to find it? For it might be something you'd hate. Why give up what is real and warm and living and lovely for what might be dead and rotten? "

He strode through the quiet village, past the warm-lighted windows of the houses and across the wind-swept marsh road to where the wooden signboard of

PAUL EMIL

the White Roe creaked and groaned as it swung ceaselessly back and forth on its bracket of rusty iron. The old men around the great fireplace gave him a courteous goodnight, watched him curiously as he climbed the stairs and then put their heads and their seamed and bearded faces, close together, talking in whispers, telling many a wild fantastic tale while the wind rattled the shutters and moaned dismally about the low-hanging eaves of the inn.

" That one did well," said Martin Theriault, the most venerable of the ancients, and the most respected since he, as a boy, had seen the Ghostly Dikemaster in the flesh. " Few escape Damase Blais; and a man would need to be a little more than human to come alive out of the Bay of Fundy on such a night as that was."

" *B'en oui,*" agreed Jean Belliveau, who also had sat by the fire the night John Gower's white face appeared at the window of the White Roe. " More than human. In league with the Powers of Darkness. It is a wonder, Isaac, that you hear no clanking of chains, no sounds from hell, in the inn at dead of night. Are there none such? "

FOG OVER FUNDY

Isaac Proux fidgetted and pulled at the string which held the black patch over his eye. He picked up the big fire-irons and straightened a blazing log of rock-maple. "I must confess, my friends, that I have heard no sounds like that. Sometimes — " He glanced up over his shoulder at the gloom shrouding the stairhead — " sometimes late he walks the floor, paces up and down like a soul in torment, and sometimes talks or reads aloud."

"Talks to his friends below," observed Floribert Gaudet. "He has money, too, eh?"

"Well," admitted Isaac, "I have seen some in the leather belt he wears. If he is in league with the devil, or if he is the devil himself, I wish some others would join up; he pays cash for everything."

"But what does he want in St. Bruno?" persisted Floribert. "He is not, and has never been, a laboring-man. One can tell that by looking at his hands."

"Well, he can work for Alphonse Trudel," said Isaac. "Why does he stay here?" The inn-keeper shrugged. "Perhaps the answer to that is riding over

PAUL EMIL

the moors tonight or playing music on the church-organ."

"She would not give up the rich Lavergne, who will be Sir Roger after the New Year — not for a man like this!"

"Who can say what that one will do?" said Isaac justly. "As well try to prophesy how the wind will blow on St. Cecilia's day as try to tell about that de Vysart."

"But this man," whispered Jean Belliveau. "You recall that night, Isaac? He spoke while he was unconscious; in his delirium he called a name. What was it, that name?"

"Candace," whispered Isaac. "That was it — Candace."

"And who or what could that be?"

"Candace?" Léandre Frechette, the littérateur of St. Bruno, coughed importantly. "Why, Candace was the name of many of the Queens of Ethiopia."

"Black ones!" said Martin Theriault triumphantly. "A black queen. That is it — Candace — "

"Candace?" The word came like a ghostly echo

FOG OVER FUNDY

from the darkness above stairs. Heads jerked around and eyes rolled upwards. John Gower stood on the stairs, his face in the shadow. They watched him as he slowly descended. His eyes, wondering, looked from face to face, into those gnarled and grizzled, nut-brown faces. He walked over to the fire. " Pardon me." He smiled at Martin Theriault. " You awakened my curiosity. It was you who spoke of Candace, was it not? Who is Candace? The name — it — it seems somehow familiar to me — Candace — "

" She was a queen of Ethiopia, m'sieur," said Martin nervously. " It — it was just something we were discussing."

" Oh, I see." John Gower laughed. " A queen of Ethiopia, eh? How interesting! Well! Forgive my inquisitiveness. I came down for some matches, M'sieur Proux, if you please."

Hastily Isaac procured a box of wax vestas and handed them to his guest. John Gower filled his pipe and lighted it. There was a great silence in the circle that usually hummed like a bee-hive. Uneasy eyes studied the fire, nervous old hands fiddled with pipestems. Presently John Gower said goodnight and once more mounted the stairs.

In his room, the same well-kept room at the head of the stairs where Armande had stopped on the night of the great storm, he sat down on the bed and rested his head on his hands, his elbows on his knees. " Candace — queer that they should be discussing — what was it? — a queen of Ethiopia. One would think — I did when they looked up at me — that they had been discussing the devil, and he walked in upon them. Queer old fellows! And a queer, quaint country too. It hasn't changed in centuries, I'm sure. Like some land one would read of in some poet's fantasy. But it's real. She is real — "

He got up and walked to the window, pulling the curtain aside to gaze out on the starry dark, on the vaguer blackness that was the sea. " I wonder what she is doing tonight — alone in that great house except for her brother — and he, from what I hear, no great company for anyone. I wish — " Wearily he turned away from the window and rubbed his hand across his brow.

FOG OVER FUNDY

" But I will see her soon. I will look in her eyes again; perhaps I shall kiss her lips and touch her hair. Nothing matters then — nothing. I shouldn't mind being the devil himself in return for such a privilege."

He looked at his ink-stained fingers, and grinned boyishly — " Cobbler, carpenter, fisherman, dike-builder, printer — what does it matter? Somehow I wish that it could be always like this. Perhaps I would ask no more. Just to be near her, to see her, to touch her — One must not be greedy. It is enough. It is more — somehow I know that — than I have ever had."

He picked up a tattered copy of the Poems of Rupert Brooke, left by the Englishman who for a while had been another enigma of the White Roe. It opened, oddly enough, at that sonnet from which Armande had quoted the night she and Marc Duclos came to minister to the victim of the storm —

" Naught broken save this body, lost but breath,
Nothing to shake the laughing heart's long peace there
But only Agony, and that has ending;
And the worst friend and enemy is but Death."

PAUL EMIL

The lines enthralled him. They were a prayer and a hope, and he said them over and over, and Elodie passing his door heard the sonorous syllables and the last words. And her face was white when she returned to the fireside and told the old men of what he spoke up there in his room. " Of Death, messieurs! The worst friend," he said, " and enemy is but Death."

At which some muttered a pious " God save us! " and others fingered the rosaries in their pockets. Truly, this was the strangest guest the White Roe had ever known, but Isaac Proux, the crafty one, knew that business would increase rather than diminish, for, like flies to a pot of treacle, the peasants would flock to his fireside in hopes of hearing strange, hair-raising tales, in hopes perhaps of seeing the very things that made them blanch and shiver.

He smiled as the company left, not one by one, but all together. He himself was not afraid: he doubted very much that the Black One would display such a huge appetite for bacon and eggs and buckwheat-pancakes as did his guest. " Anyway," mused Isaac with the good inn-keeper's philosophy, " he pays well."

FOG OVER FUNDY

Ulric did not leave his room next day. His meals were brought there to him. Armande, passing the locked door, saw in it a symbol of what stood between her and him. It came to her that the must and corruption that had begun to attack the ancient house, had worked their way, too, with Ulric's spirit, eating like some numbing canker far into him, atrophying the strong impulses, the noble purposes that must surely at one time have been latent within him. " He does not care," she thought. " He does not seem to want to care and I fear it will be a bitter task to make him. But he is a man. It is a man's place to lead."

She thought of Leon, of how, had he been here, the great halls would have rung with his hearty, soldier's laughter, the stairways echoed to his nimble feet. Quick as a flash, Leon had been, in his speech, in his actions; utterly intolerant of the things that Ulric paid no attention to — slipshod ways, neglect of surroundings. And Leon had loved Beausejour; not, she thought with a wan smile, in such a way as would hold him to it, but in his fashion. He would have come, she knew, gladly, had he ever dreamed there was need of him. But now

PAUL EMIL

he would come no more. And perhaps that uncompromising dark-panelled door would never be really opened to her, would stand strong between her and the things she hoped to do.

All day it snowed and the mercury dropped steadily. The thermometer in the stable-yard, she saw, when towards evening she went to visit Feu Follet showed twenty below zero, and in that spot it was sheltered from the cruel blasts of the north wind. Windows were caked thick and hard with frost, its terrible tension almost visible on the wood of window sash, on the iron latch of the stable door. But Feu Follet was warm and snug in her box and Hervé tramped around, watchful, in his comfortable room above in the loft.

Late in the evening the snow ceased and the wind abated; the stars shone out like small, bright spearpoints, hard, cruel, metallic. The frost-tortured trees in the park cracked with the sharp, staccato sounds of rifle fire and the bitter cold against one's face was a concrete, a tangible thing. People stayed indoors, hugging their firesides. The world was utterly still, like a dead world. Late, the telephone at Beausejour gave its

FOG OVER FUNDY

soft, slow ring. The girl Claudette answered and came presently to knock on Armande's door. "It is for you, Mademoiselle Armande — the Doctor Duclos."

Wondering, Armande left her warm chair by the hearth, left her book and the recumbent Sirdar. Strange that Marc should call her at such an hour on such a night. He wasn't given to such tricks. There must be some sound and excellent reason.

"Armande!" His voice was urgent, very grave. "You must come at once. It is Suzanne Delagarde. Pneumonia. And her heart is no good. She asks for you. I am speaking from Camille Brun's house across the road from her cottage. Can you come at once?"

"At once, Marc."

She dressed herself, muffled herself in a knitted habitant scarf and a great riding coat. She routed Hervé out of bed and Feu Follet, eager in spite of the terrible cold, was made ready; then, through the flying snow, sharp and stinging as needle points, she rode to St. Bruno, the steam rising in great clouds from the big mare's body, the white snow, spurned by her flying hoofs, rising in vapoury clouds. Past the church, over

PAUL EMIL

the bare planks of the covered bridge with a thunder of hoof-beats, into the village, past the sleep-wrapped cottages, their windows glistening whitely.

At Camille Brun's she left Feu Follet to be warmly stabled and ran through the snow to Suzanne Delagarde's cottage, its windows glowing softly, on the edge of the ice-rimmed sea. Cruel and bitter, she thought, to die on such a night: how much easier the passing when the skies were blue and warm, when the birds sang softly and the voice of the sea was low and gentle, not the angry muttering and crashing that came from it now.

Marc opened the door — Marc looking very young and undoctorlike in a blue sweater and trousers of ancient tweed — Marc who turned stolidly away from the well-appointed, glistening hospital-rooms to spend his life in the humble cottages of the peasants, giving gladly of his hard-won knowledge, his tremendous skill, for little or no reward that man could see.

"There is little time," he whispered, his eyes dark and earnest, looking into hers. "It is a cruel thing, this. She has been raving. She speaks of strange things. You know, perhaps, something of what she will say to you?"

"It is — about the little boy, Paul Emil."

"Yes."

"About — about Leon."

"Yes. He was her husband —"

"But how?"

"Gregoire Delagarde was a brute. She loved Leon. But she was good. She would have gone on. Then Gregoire was drowned. They never found him. She and Leon were secretly married. They did not wait — why should they? He was going away. Then the boy came early. That I know. No one thought anything but that he belonged to Gregoire. She would not talk. She feared you would want to claim the child, take it from her."

"That was why — she seemed to dislike me —"

"Come."

Quietly, Marc holding her hand, they went into the room where Suzanne lay, the look of death upon her face. The eyes that stared up into Armande's were huge, were bright and alive with the fever that was upon her — bright with a too-great brightness that must soon grow dim.

PAUL EMIL

Armande knelt by the bed, touched the hot, wasted hand on the coverlet, whispered, "Suzanne!"

Suzanne's gaze did not leave her face. "*Mon p'tit garçon* — Her voice was a rasping whisper. " Mine and Leon's — you know."

" I know, my sister."

Suzanne's lips smiled. " You — will be good to him? I am sorry — I feared to lose him. I loved him so."

" I love him too. I will be good to him — as to my own. And God will be good to you, my dear."

" Thank you." The whisper was fainter, farther off. " Oh, thank you, my lady."

Armande turned her head away, her lips hard shut, her eyes swimming. She saw Marc, his unruly head bent, his lips moving in prayer — Marc, who could bring in prayer so honestly when all science was as nothing. Suzanne's eyes were closed. Her breath came short and hard.

Armande got up. Her hand clasped Marc's arm. He shook his head.

" The boy," whispered Armande. " Where is he? "

" She said goodby to him. I sent him away, over to

FOG OVER FUNDY

Camille Brun's. I could not have him here. I could not stand — more of it. She is happy now. You have made her happy. She can go in peace. The curé was here. He had to go on to Cormier's Cove — the old Julie, too, has chosen this night to go. It's an awful, a strange and beautiful thing — Death. Such misery you see, but, too, such great peace, such great hope, such boundless trust. It makes you think, makes you know that people are good, Armande — that life is good."

" You could never become hardened to Death, Marc."

" No. No — why should I? This — " He gestured towards the bed — " tears my heart. It must always tear my heart, but it is good for the spirit; like a cleansing draught. She will have great peace soon. She will be better off than we. Let us pray for her — it is all one can do now."

And they prayed, silently, standing there side-by-side, and a great peace seemed to come into the room and settle there, and to their listening ears there seemed to come, far, far off, the murmur and rustle and beat of great wings that grew louder and louder, then as swiftly died away.

PAUL EMIL

Paul Emil sat between Marc and Armande, his head, the golden curls imprisoned under a red knitted toque, resting against her shoulder. He was quiet, but not sleepy; solemn but not frightened. He knew his mother had gone away, that she would not come back, that in some vaguely visioned, far off day he would see her again and she would once more take him by the hand, for in his dreaming, it seemed that, when the day came, he would still be a little boy as he was now, and she would be the same as he had known her.

But he was happy enough now, sitting in Dr. Marc's big car between the doctor and the lovely lady herself. It was such a joy as he had never even dared to hope would come to him; and, still greater bliss, he was going to stay with her tonight, going to live for a while at the big gray house at which he had often stared with round, wondering eyes, which loomed so huge in his child's mind that he thought it very likely indeed a little fellow like him might easily become lost in its vast halls and labyrinthine ways, were she not there to watch out for him.

Armande had asked to take him home with her tonight, and Marc had agreed. Kindly neighbors filled the little cottage. They had marvelled to see Armande there. They had looked curiously, some darkly, at her. Nothing was said, nothing would be said, for some time, about Suzanne's confession. Marc, knowing his people, knew it was better so. They would not understand. They would think less of the dead girl, whom now they wept and prayed for; they would think less of the little boy, now that he was no longer one of them. They would blame Suzanne for giving herself, even in marriage, to Leon de Vysart, almost before the cruel waters had closed over Gregoire Delagarde: no matter that Gregoire was a blackguard and had treated her most miserably.

Even in the house of death there were whisperings and speculations and dark things bruited about. This was the work of the Moon Witch. She had coveted the child. She had hated Suzanne for wanting to keep Paul Emil away from her evil influence. So she had put a spell upon Suzanne, and Suzanne was dead. They did not want to see her take the child away; they thought it should be prevented, but they dared not interfere.

PAUL EMIL

There was nothing they could do. Useless to appeal to Dr. Duclos or to the curé; the one would chide them and laugh at them, the other would threaten them with hell-fire and assorted curses if they didn't cease their superstitious talk and belief.

"But why should she come to stand at Suzanne's deathbed?" demanded Anna Gaudet, cousin of Elodie of the White Roe. "It does not seem right. Suzanne did not like her. I have seen Suzanne go out of her way to avoid a meeting with that one, and always she cautioned Paul Emil against her. Now the witch is the last one to see her on earth and carries off the boy before one has time to sneeze."

"He should be with one of his own kind, Anna; that is right enough," agreed Camille Brun's wife. "But he was with us and I tell you it was no joke. He cannot get along with other children. He would not talk with mine or play with them — just sat in a corner with his chin on his hand and a queer look in those big eyes of his."

"A spell," said Anna vehemently. "The boy has been bewitched. Always, he seemed like a changeling. She will bring him up to serve the Powers of Darkness. It is a sin — a terrible sin to see this going on under our noses with that poor thing lying there, her soul scarcely arrived in purgatory."

"What is a sin?" The deep voice of Père Archambeault made them all jump guiltily. Anna and Sophie Brun and Artemise Gallant and the rest, sitting around the kitchen stove. The white-haired, hawk-nosed priest walked into the room, his black sugar-loaf hat in his frost-numbed fingers, a long coat of ancient mode buttoned to his chin. Under tufted, shaggy white brows, his eyes glowed like living coals. "What were you speaking of, Anna Gaudet?"

"Of young Paul Emil, *mon père*," simpered Anna. "The — Mademoiselle de Vysart has taken him home with her. One says she will keep him for good."

"That would be well," said the curé. "An excellent thing for the little fellow. But did I not hear you speak of spells, and of Powers of Darkness?"

"Suzanne did not like the de Vysart."

"That has nothing to do with Paul Emil," said the curé decisively. "Place a guard upon your lips that they say nothing wrong, my children; and pray for God's

PAUL EMIL

light in your hearts that no evil may enter therein. Must I tell you forever, in vain, that God frowns upon this black superstition, that it is a sin to believe in the pagan things that I well know you still discuss. What would you be saying now — that Armande de Vysart has the Evil Eye? God give you all eyes as clear and bright and shining with the light of heaven as hers are — that is my prayer for you. I baptized her as I baptized many of you; I saw her grow; I prepared her for confirmation. Because her ways are not your ways, do you condemn her? I tell you, cast out these evils from your hearts or God will punish you."

The good man stalked out of the kitchen and went in to kneel and pray from his gentle heart for the soul of her, departed; for the little boy left alone, for light that should be given to those who live in darkness, light to see the beauty in a young girl's soul where their wicked minds saw only evil. But prayers are not too strong against the superstitions of the ages. A grim and unrepentant silence followed the curé's exit from the kitchen. Then Anna Gaudet said, " He too has fallen under her spell. She has bewitched him."

FOG OVER FUNDY

Marc Duclos said good-night to Armande and Paul Emil and drove away, chains clanking softly in the snow. "We are home, Paul Emil, *mon brave!*" said Armande, taking his hand as they climbed the steps. "We shall have great fun here together, you and I, *hein?*" She heard the engine of another car, saw lights swing around the house from the garage. "How is this? Our car. And so late!"

She led Paul Emil into the house, into the dimness of the hall. Only one light burned there and in its poor radiance she did not see Ulric, a bag in each hand, coming down the stairs. He had stopped, stood motionless, at sight of her. He looked as if he would turn around and go back. His eyes were furtive.

Armande sized him up. She did not need to question him; she knew. "It is flight, Ulric," she said calmly. "It is desertion."

"It — well, what of it! I'm going. There's nothing to keep me."

"There is nothing left, Ulric?"

He did not answer. "I had guessed it." She nodded slowly. "I did not want to believe it. I hated myself

PAUL EMIL

for thinking such a thought, for entertaining the idea that my brother could be a — "

" You do not need to suffer."

" No, I suppose not. You thought, with Leon gone, and Armande married to Roger Lavergne, all would be well for you."

" You could never do the sensible thing. Even now it isn't too late. You'll have to do it, you'll have to do something."

" The place is still — ours? "

" That — and nothing else."

" That will have to do."

" But you are insane! You must be. You can't do anything by yourself. You can't stay here alone."

" God is good, Ulric. And kind. And He takes one thing away, only to give back something better. This is Leon's son."

" Leon's — " Ulric stared at Paul Emil, who stared in turn at the red-faced giant in the great coonskin coat, a giant he did not like because, it was clear, the giant was not good to his lady.

" It is impossible! This boy — I've seen him in the

FOG OVER FUNDY

village. I have it — Gregoire Delagarde's son."

"Look at him, Ulric. I have seen Leon in his face, in his eyes, in his very step, these several years. It is so. They were married. Tonight I learned the story. The girl is — gone away."

Ulric walked down the remaining steps. He looked at the little boy guiltily. He could not look at Armande. "I thought you were abed," he muttered. "I — I thought to avoid this."

"There is nothing, Ulric. I have nothing to say. You can go in peace."

"That's just it!" He burst out, almost crying. "Your unbelievable cold-bloodedness! Your infernal aplomb! You — you'd think it meant nothing — nothing at all to me — "

"Well, does it?"

He brushed past her and went out, leaving the door open behind him. With Paul Emil, big eyed, at her side she saw Ulric get in the car and Hervé drove away. She watched the tail lights' red reflection on the snow, watched them vanish down the road. He would take the train at Sackville. She thought of rats that scurry away

PAUL EMIL

from a doomed ship. She wanted to despise Ulric, to rage against him, but she found she could only pity him for his weakness.

She closed the door, slipped the old-fashioned bolt in its place and fastened the chain. She looked down at Paul Emil and smiled. He smiled shyly back at her. She touched his curls, told him to take off his coat and his overshoes.

"M'sieur Ulric—" Paul Emil looked up from a tussle with one shoe—"he goes away for a long time?"

"For a long time."

"Not because I come here?"

"No, child." Armande laughed through her tears. "He did not know you were coming. But now, you see, he can stay away and not worry at all about me, for you will be here to look after me."

"I can." He straightened up bravely, squaring his shoulders under the little fawn jersey, his eyes very earnest. "Still," he said doubtfully, "he was such a great big man and I am so small yet. Still I could fight for you, Ma'm'selle Armande."

FOG OVER FUNDY

"I know you could." She knelt and gathered him into her arms. "I know you could; you are very brave. And I may need you to fight for me."

A fire burned in the living-room, warm and bright. "Come, Paul Emil, we will sit there for just a little while, then you can go to bed. It is very late."

He marched proudly beside her and sat on a hassock by her chair. They watched the leaping flames and the shadows flickering, dancing on the wall, and they smiled at each other and did not speak. By-and-by his head rested against her knee, the tired eyes closed, and he slept. Hungrily she gazed into his face and thought exultantly, "I am not alone. I shall never be alone now."

CHAPTER VIII

THREE WHO LOVED HER

MONSIEUR Lorenzo Frenette, advocate and notary, sat back in a leather easy chair in the library of Beausejour, juxtaposed the fingertips of his well-kept left hand to those of his right, looked over the gold rim of the pince-nez perched on his thin beak of a nose, coughed deeply and said, " So, Mademoiselle Armande, it will be clear to you from what I have said — having thoroughly investigated the affairs of your family — that poverty, no less, stares you in the face. Your assets, beyond the house and the lands adjoining — dubious assets, I may say, at that — are quite, quite negligible. Your brother was most unfortunate, most indiscreet, in the management of affairs. My advice to you is that you sell the property for what it will bring — not much, I fear, in the present deplorable state of the market — and then look about you."

FOG OVER FUNDY

"I would never sell the place, M'sieur Frenette. Never! That is out of the question." Armande was perched on the edge of the great walnut table, gazing down at the elongated lawyer.

"But, my dear child, what else is there for you?"

"I can make money out of the farm. Any one who will work can make money out of it—"

"But a girl like you!" Monsieur Frenette shrugged and spread his hands wide. "A lady like you!"

Armande smiled. "Is work incompatible with being a lady? I think not. I was living in a fool's paradise, though for a long time I have known that things were not at all as they should be. Now that I know how bad they are, I can go ahead. I shall borrow money. I shall have a farm here. I won't have it said that it was with me the name of de Vysart died from the Tantramar."

The notary stood up straight and bowed low from the waist. His spectacles glistened in the morning sunlight. "I salute you, mademoiselle. I salute the blood, the breeding, the courage you stand for. You are taking, let me tell you again, a tremendous load upon such slender shoulders, but if strength of will and purpose

THREE WHO LOVED HER

will accomplish the trick, then it is done."

"Thank you, m'sieur. It shall be done."

She spoke bravely, but after she had seen Frenette to the door and watched him drive off in his tiny coupe, she returned to the library and stared thoughtfully into the flames. So often she had meditated upon the proud strength of her house, on the brave men and women who had borne the name since first the fleur-de-lys waved upon the battlements of Quebec and Port Royal; so often had she exulted in being one of them, with the same faith, the same high ideals and purpose inflexible. Never had it occurred to her that one day it might devolve upon her, alone, unsupported, to keep the faith, to carry on the strong tradition. But the day had come. Leon dead, Ulric ignominiously fled, she alone was left.

The library door opened softly. Paul Emil's bright head was poked in and he gazed questioningly at her. "There," she thought, "is my ally. There is the only de Vysart left to me. A stout fellow." She smiled at him and beckoned. "Come in, *mon brave;* do not hesitate. You are free to come and go as you will in this house. No door will ever be closed to you."

FOG OVER FUNDY

He came in; walked over and stood beside her. "One door was closed. I would have asked you to go in there," he said in his quaint English, "but you were with M'sieur Frenette, the *notaire*."

She thought: "It is Leon's room he speaks of. Leon's — "

"I went there." His eyes shone. "Such a lovely room that was! There were guns and soldier hats and pictures of great airships, and silver cups and many books and a hundred other things. And pictures of a man there — a soldier. Who was that man? Was he a very brave one?"

"Very brave indeed, Paul Emil. He flew in those airships you saw. He was in many wars. He was strong."

"Then I shall be like him, *Tante* Armande."

"You will be like him. Without a doubt you will, when you grow up, be as good and as brave a man as he was."

"Where is he now?"

"Heaven."

"Ah, he is with *maman*. In heaven. That is a good place, but it is not so nice for ones like us, to be left behind."

THREE WHO LOVED HER

She knew he missed Suzanne, missed her more now than he had in the first week after her going. Her own kindness to him, her gentleness and love, could make up to him for much, in time perhaps for everything; but sometimes now when he sat alone, when he thought she did not see, his little mouth would tremble and the blue eyes blink away their tears.

"Paul Emil," she said, "you and I have the great task of running this house and farm. We are to be farmers, to work hard, to have hens and cows and big fat hogs. We shall be very busy people, Paul Emil. Of course, we shall have Fidèle to help us, but we are the bosses, you and I."

He nodded very seriously. "*Bien!*" he said. "I will help you the best I can."

"I ask no more. But now you must set about your lessons. To be a good farmer you must study very hard."

He marched off, hiding his reluctance. Much pleasanter to talk with her, who had made him call her *tante*, much more to his liking to sit beside her and gaze at her. Nothing, he thought, could be more lovely than she

FOG OVER FUNDY

was, or more kind. But she was sad sometimes, he knew, and lonely; and at those times she would mount her great horse and ride away for miles. When he was bigger he, too, would have a horse and ride with her. He did not like to think of her being alone. There should be someone, big and strong, like the soldier in the picture in that room whose mystery had intrigued him, who could slay dragons and giants and ward off all dangers that might beset her.

The danger, for instance, of the Black One, of whom the children spoke in school. The Black One, sometimes they called him l'Etranger, dwelt at the Inn of the White Roe and had come up out of the depths of the sea the night of the terrible storm. It was she, one said, who had first greeted the Black One when he came upon the land. And now the two of them went together and roamed over the marshes at night and in the churchyard among the tombstones.

It was not her choice or her doing, reasoned Paul Emil. They said she could put spells on people and make people do what she wanted them to. They called her the Moon Witch and said she could turn the great

THREE WHO LOVED HER

white hound into a black cat and ride through the air on a broomstick. Often he had heard this and always he wondered, but never had he dared to speak of it to her, for fear she should do it and fly away and he'd never see her again.

Armande, at that moment, would have been most glad of a few supernatural powers — that of changing marsh mud into gold-dust perhaps, or straw into banknotes or, above all, of transforming a thing that seemed monstrous in its evil to that which would be good and right. But no such powers were vouchsafed to her. There was poverty, there was a hard future, there was a love that, though sweet beyond all dreaming, held no hope of happiness, no prospect of fulfillment. John Gower worked each day and often at night in the dingy little printing shop of Alphonse Trudel. She did not see John Gower, she avoided the places where he might see her. She suffered in her heart, remembering moments of high ecstasy, fraught with beauty and tenderness — moments that were, that must have been, lies.

She must put away her dreams now, it seemed; must come out of that make-believe world, that wondrous

FOG OVER FUNDY

realm, in which all her life she had wandered. Now the moon would be just the moon, not a thing of magic in whose light, enchanting, faery things were disclosed; the far-sweeping marshlands with their rampart dikes no more would be plains of mystery with glamour in every blade of grass; Feu Follet from being a golden winged steed would become just a splendid mare on which to ride about drab errands. By night, the great organ that her father had presented to the church in St. Bruno, would remain forever silent and if music should come to the passing wayfarer in the dark watches, it would indeed be ghostly music played by a wraith of the girl that used to sit at the console.

Days and nights now she spent trying to put some order into the chaos Ulric had left — a hopeless-seeming, wretched task. So many things would have to go — the car, the horses and hounds Ulric had kept. The servants had gone already, save the boy Hervé, who was most loyal to Armande and who lent his best powers willingly to any task. Long hours were spent with Fidèle Thibodeau, who tenanted the home farm over the hill, who, used to having his own way these many years un-

THREE WHO LOVED HER

der Ulric's careless regime, was neither quick nor willing to take orders from a mere girl. Her ambitious schemes for stock- and poultry-raising he met with stolid skepticism; to him hens and pigs were merely hens and pigs, and were not made of gold as this bright-eyed, eager girl seemed to think. Of course, he would do what she bade him, but — After that came a shrug, signifying much or nothing.

Two weeks after Ulric had gone, when Armande, with Paul Emil, had settled down to a quieter, more serious existence, when the marsh-country and all the Acadian land was blanketed five feet deep in snow, and zero night with bitter monotony followed zero night, when the moon and stars shone upon a dead and silent world, Roger Lavergne came to Beausejour.

He came at night, unheralded. Armande opened the door at his summons, and when she saw him standing there, so tall, so assured, his sleek dark head bared, his cap of black Persian-lamb crushed in his hand, a great gladness, a surge of relief rose in her heart and, for a moment, there possessed her a temptation, amounting to an urge, to throw herself in his arms, to

FOG OVER FUNDY

yield, to cling to him. It would be so easy, it would be so right. It would put an end to all these worries, to all these doubts and fears; it would solve the seemingly unsolvable future. The bright way beckoned, radiant with light, bordered by lovely flowers, with summer all the way. With agony in her heart, with a prayer unvoiced, she fought it from her. For what? Only God and something deeper in her heart than she had ever gone, could tell her that.

She said: " Roger! I am so glad to see you. So happy that you have come." He embraced her lightly; silent, but saying with his eyes a thousand words of hope, of love and gladness. She drew him into the hall, into the great living-room where the fire blazed cheerily, where Paul Emil rose quickly, defensively from his little chair by the hearth-side and bowed his bright head when Roger said to him: " How now, Paul Emil? Have you proven a good protector to Mademoiselle Armande? Have you slain all the giants and cut the tails off all the dragons who sought to attack her? " He struggled out of his coat and, walking over, held out his hand to the boy. Paul Emil took it gravely.

THREE WHO LOVED HER

"I have not had occasion to do those things, as yet, m'sieur."

"But you would be ready, in case, eh?" He turned to Armande, looked at her gravely, smilingly — Armande in the worn breeks of Bedford cord, the shiny boots, the high-necked sweater and brown tweed coat. "Still the same Armande," he said softly. "A little quieter, a little weary perhaps?"

"I think not, Roger." She smiled at him brightly. "But — it is somewhat different here."

"Yes; I can imagine. I did what I could — for Ulric." He frowned at the fire. "It was all very hopeless."

She knew suddenly that he had ceased to help Ulric in the hope of hastening the inevitable, with the idea of forcing her hand. She did not despise him for it nor think less of him. His ways were subtle, yet they were the ways of the strong. Anyway, Ulric had been beyond helping.

"I know," she said, sitting on the arm of the divan, absently fishing in her jacket pocket for one of the cigarettes that were wont to roll about there. She found none. Roger stepped over with his case. She took one, took his light, thanked him with her eyes. " Ulric — he is with you now? "

"He works on one of the papers. He knows much about dogs and horses, and can be of use to us."

" He does not fight against life, against fate, against anything. He will never fight."

" Perhaps he is wise." Roger's voice was low and very earnest. " It is the better part of wisdom, *chère,* not to take arms against the inevitable."

" Nothing save death is inevitable," she countered stubbornly.

" Nothing? " The dark brows went up. " This, from you, is heresy. This contradicts all your philosophy — " He waved his cigarette — " At least insofar as I know your philosophy. Is not love, true love, inevitable? "

She bit her lip. He was so skilled a swordsman in himself; with a knowledge of his opponent's weaknesses he was all but invincible.

" The coming of true love is inevitable, yes, I believe that; one's yielding to it — no."

" Ah, you distinguish — you to whom true love has never come. Or has it, since last I met you? "

THREE WHO LOVED HER

She saw the coarse red paw of Ulric in this, Ulric in his cups, talking, babbling to a faintly contemptuous, all attentive Roger. Ulric telling of John Gower, of their meetings at the church, their walks under the moon, the gossip of the villagers.

"I shall take Paul Emil up to his bed now," she said. "You will excuse us."

Roger bowed. Paul Emil put down his primer and, rising, bowed to Roger. "Good night, m'sieur."

"Good night, Paul Emil." Roger bowed sedately. In his eyes was a look, pensive, admiring, as he watched them, side by side, the straight proud figure of Armande, the sturdy little form of Leon de Vysart's son, pass through the wide doorway and climb the great staircase. In this moment, he knew better his love for her, for her splendid courage, her pride. He felt humble before her. He felt that she, beleaguered by poverty, alone, frail in body, was stronger than he in the utter honesty of her heart, the directness of her purpose.

When, presently, she returned, he said, "Won't you switch off the lights and let us sit by the fire? It is so I remember you most happily, Armande — in the firelight."

Silently she put out the lights and took the chair facing him. Hands clasped in front of him, for a while he did not speak but looked into the flamy caverns as if to read there what should guide him best. Armande, too, kept silent, not that she was at a loss for what to say, simply that she knew what must be said and that it was not for her to say it.

"Of course, you know why I have come," he said at last, glancing quickly at her, seeing the warm light in her hair, in her eyes, admiring the long symmetry of her body, at ease in the great leather chair. "It is not that I wish to irk you with my pleading or say that which might be distasteful to you. Simply, it seemed to me that now, leaving the question of love out of it — of your love for me — you would consider accepting what I offer you, what with all my heart I want you to have. Everything I am and have can be yours, Armande. Think! What is there here for you? What can there ever be? You have some fine visions, a noble purpose, but what you undertake is all too much for you

THREE WHO LOVED HER

alone. Why do you choose this dark, hard road when there is a bright and easy one before you?"

"When I saw you standing there tonight, I asked myself that same question."

"And?"

She shook her head slowly. "Something I cannot name. Something that is too deep in me for me to know. Looking at it calmly, Roger, I know I am a fool to turn away from a man like you, to refuse the splendid things you offer me."

"It is not for Marc Duclos?"

"Poor Marc. No, it is not for him."

"Then — for this other?"

She did not answer. She knew that Roger had struck it, unerringly, as he was bound to. She knew that, had John Gower never come up out of the sea, had his eyes never looked so wistfully into hers or his lips not brought her ecstasy, she might have gone with Roger Lavergne tonight; she might not have been able to resist all the decent and reasonable arguments that Roger could put forth. She might have chosen the sane, the easy road, not this rough and unknown way in which one could not

FOG OVER FUNDY

see even one's hand outstretched. But John Gower stood beside her chair; his face, thin, white, earnest, was bent down to her; those eyes of his in which lurked, behind the utter joy of beholding her, some dread, some formless fear, held her eyes, and his whispered words, " I love you," were in her heart, so that almost she said aloud to this vision, " I believe."

" Ulric told me of that. He spoke of your being with this man, of your saying that love—" Roger's voice was harsh.

" Yes, I spoke of love."

" You love him— this stranger, this nobody! "

" It must be love, Roger. It is something I have never known before. And I have known many happinesses. None like this. It transforms the whole world, it makes one breathe a different air, it makes all things enchanting."

" But — but — well, you were always strange, Armande; always the one to do mad things, but even I, who studied you lovingly and thought I knew you well, never dreamed of anything like this. And what of this love? Where does it lead? "

THREE WHO LOVED HER

"I cannot tell you. I do not know."

"You go on blindly, not knowing, not caring!"

"Not knowing, yes; but not caring — oh, there you are wrong, Roger. I care very much, but I go on in darkness, in the deepest darkness. I have no light; only faith, to guide me. That is what I find so beautiful about love, that is why I know this must indeed be love — one questions nothing, one asks so little —"

"Love! This is madness!"

"But are they not very closely related, love and madness? Aren't persons in love just a little mad? Or a great deal?"

"I must see this man."

A shadow seemed to flit across her face. "Why should you wish to see him?"

"To find out, perhaps, the secret of his power to fascinate. If one could learn that, it might prove more valuable than the Philosopher's Stone."

"I wish you would not, Roger. It can do no good. It will only —" The bell in the hall tinkled softly. She looked apprehensively at Roger. He smiled. "Shall I go? It is dark —"

FOG OVER FUNDY

"Thank you, no. I'll go myself."

Fearful, praying that it might be Marc Duclos, or Frenette the lawyer, or the curé, she went to the door.

"Armande," he said, "I had to come. I stayed away as long as I could. I — why do I never see you now? Is there something — some reason — ?"

She lowered her gaze, seemed as if she would dismiss him; then said, "Won't you come in for a while? There is only Roger Lavergne here — a friend of — of our family's."

"I would not intrude —" Behind him was the icy backdrop of snow and star-pointed sky.

"Come," she said, and led the way to the fireside. Briefly she introduced them.

"We met," said Roger, "the day after your descent — or should I say ascent — upon St. Bruno. You were not very well."

"No." John Gower sat in a chair Armande had placed for him beyond the ring of brightest light. "I was in pretty bad shape, at that time. I did not properly realize how much Mademoiselle de Vysart had done for me. Afterwards I learned it was a great deal."

THREE WHO LOVED HER

"It would take a lifetime, no doubt, to repay," said Roger dryly.

"All of that; though I do not think she wants anything in the way of repayment."

"About women, one never knows. And our women are different, in some things, from those of your great country. They are, I should say, more serious; more likely to take things to heart — "

"I can not say — about the women of my country."

"No? You did not know any. Come — "

John Gower laughed. "It would be hard to explain. It would be dull."

"I wonder." Roger smiled. "Well, your reticence is becoming. You must like it here in St. Bruno?"

"Yes. I like it immensely."

The conversation languished. Roger was perfectly at ease and John Gower did not seem at all disturbed. Only Armande showed signs of restlessness, and presently the Stranger got up from his chair. "It is time I was on my way," he said quietly, but there was something in his voice that made them both look at him. He said it as if he meant a long way. Armande's eyes were

FOG OVER FUNDY

troubled. Roger was startled at what he saw in her face — something that might be called fear, in one who was fearless; some deep concern.

"You do not stay long," she said as if urging him to linger, when, only a few minutes ago, she had seemed as if his going would be most welcome.

"It has been pleasant," he said. He nodded to Roger. Armande walked with him out into the hall. Her hand fell on his as he turned the doorknob; her eyes looked up into his and saw there misery and weariness and defeat.

"Why do you look like that? Is it — is it because I seemed unkind to you? Oh, do you not understand —"

"I try to," he answered. "But there is so much —" He stopped, gazed at her long. "You are so lovely, so dear. I — there is no sense in my being here; there was no sense in my doing what I did — staying here, haunting you, forcing myself upon you. It was all madness — now I'm paying for it."

"What about me, m'sieur?"

He turned away. "I hope to God you do not suffer. You are wise, anyway; you have some sense where I

THREE WHO LOVED HER

have none. You did not let me see you — "

"Do you — think that was of my choosing? If it was hard for you to do without a sight of me, do you think that to me it was less hard — ? "

"Then why — why did you shut yourself up here? I know you did."

"You make it difficult for me — very difficult."

"I know." He opened the door. " It is all very wrong, but you mean so much to me. I'd risk anything, do anything, just to see you and be near you. Now goodnight."

"Goodnight. When you said, ' I must be on my way,' you did not mean — the long road."

He nodded. " This that I travel is a *cul-de-sac* perhaps. I thought that in you I had found the end of all worthwhile roads."

"Do you not still think so? "

"Always; but I am not worthy to come to you. I am nothing — less than nothing."

"No! " She pressed his hand tightly. " Do not say that. Do not think that."

He lifted her hand to his lips and kissed it and walked out into the frosty dark. She heard his footsteps crunch-

FOG OVER FUNDY

ing crisply down the drive. She closed the door and went back to the fire where Roger was still sitting. For a while they were silent, each watching the fire where a blazing beech-log broke and fell in a shower of tiny sparks. John Gower's going seemed to have left a gap, a void, of which he, no less than Armande was very much aware.

"Strange sort of fellow," he said finally. "I could not see him very well, but there seemed to be something oddly familiar about his face — as if I had seen it often. Who is he or what, beyond being a sailor? Or is he really a sailor? There's some mystery here; I can sense that."

"Mystery?" Armande shrugged. "If there is a mystery then it is as hidden to me as to everyone else. I know nothing at all about him — he has told me nothing."

"And you have not been curious? You have not tried to find out — ?"

"Curious — yes, I've been curious. But I have not tried to find out. I have accepted him for what he is — just a man, a stranger. I have been kind to him."

THREE WHO LOVED HER

"More than kind, Armande."

She held up her hand. "It is all much ado about nothing, Roger."

"Then — then you feel it will lead nowhere?"

"Nowhere," she said miserably. "What — what hope is there? What — oh, it is all so futile, so impossible. I will not talk of it."

"Then let us talk of brighter things. Perhaps talking about them will make you want them again, and you will consent to come with me, out of this land of ice and darkness."

They talked then of other days, of hours that had been gay and happy, of visits she had made to his home when she and his sister were fellow-students at the Sault. He made her laugh, he made her forget for just a little while, and she was glad. But at the end of the evening he was no farther ahead than when he had come. He knew it. He stood up, refusing courteously her invitation to stay the night. "It would do no good. It would make my going still harder. To sit here and look at you and hear your voice, to lose myself in dreams, then to awaken and realize that you are not

FOG OVER FUNDY

for me — I cannot bear it, Armande. I must go. But I will be always with you, always yours — "

" You are too kind to me, Roger — too noble. You must not think of me or bother with me. Best to forget, to take your own happiness in a world that offers you so much. It is strange that you, with all the world to choose from, should come to this forgotten place and — and want me — "

" The loveliest gems have not yet been discovered, my dear. They are hidden in the distant mountains, in the jungles, in the depths of the sea. Now I must go. Adieu." He lifted her hand and pressed it with his lips. " I shall write and you must write."

They walked into the hall. Outside, a motor roared as Hervé warmed it against the frozen night. She watched Roger go down the steps and get in beside Hervé. She saw him wave and waved to him in reply; then the car rolled down the drive and the soft thrumming of its exhaust died on her ears and its glowing lights upon her eyes. She shivered, feeling alone and depressed. She went back to the fire and put more wood upon it and sat there for long hours, dreaming.

THREE WHO LOVED HER

She could not delude herself about Roger. He was not a man to be misprized, not the sort a girl could turn away from without regret. He was hurt, and his hurt would go deep. The world could not see behind that suave and smiling mask of his brown face nor ever imagine that he, destined always for the high places, could suffer a grievous wound from a girl so obscure as she. He took it lightly. He was not affronted that she should prefer the love of some nameless wanderer to his own. Only the loss of her, the loss of hope, could hurt him. And he, in his fashion, when he went away, had looked as dejected and forlorn as the stranger.

John Gower, too, would go away. They would all go from her, as Leon had gone, and Ulric. She had seen it in John Gower's eyes, in his speech, in the signals of hopelessness and defeat. Well, let him go. It was the best, the only thing. Let him go, with no word more, into the oblivion from which he had come. Still, for her, she knew, his spirit would haunt the Tantramar and if ever again she walked the white roads under the moon or sat before the organ in St. Bruno's Church, he would be there at her side, his dark eyes pleading.

FOG OVER FUNDY

She stirred from these musings. The fire had burned low. It was a mass of crimson and black; its light was very soft, very gentle. In the hall, the old clock struck a solemn one. The night-wind rattled the shutters. Time for bed. She stood up. The long, searching beams of a car's headlights moved along the wall. It would be Hervé returning. But no, the car stopped at the front door. She went quickly. It would be Marc, no doubt. Who else at this late hour? But why Marc?

He came quickly up the steps and followed her into the house. He was pale, excited, his eyes strangely bright. "I am so glad you were still up. Tonight I had to see you — to know what to do? First I thought of the police, the Mounties; it will in the end be a job for them. Then I thought I would come direct to you."

Armande straightened from putting wood on the fire. Her cheeks were white in the flaring light of the crackling bark. Her lips were parted; her hands clenched tight. Marc had flung himself into the chair where Roger had been sitting, but got out of it immediately and stood, legs apart, staring at the fire.

"What is it all about, Marc?"

THREE WHO LOVED HER

"I find it hard now to tell you, Armande. It is harder than I thought. You love this man, this one who calls himself John Gower?"

"Yes." It was barely audible. "Yes, that is so."

"Well, then! Only tonight, as I looked over some old papers that had come to me from New York, I saw his picture. He is not John Gower, he is not a sailor — he is the man who killed Leon!"

He looked at her, thinking to see horror and astonishment and worse, in her eyes, in her face. He saw none of these things. She had seated herself on a chair-arm, her shoulders slumped a little, her hands clasped. She made no sign.

"But — but are you not — !" He stared at her in wonderment. "Not surprised, not — "

"No." She stood up wearily. "I have known that for some time, Marc. Oh, not — believe me — at the time I — I fell in love with him. It was afterward, after the harm had been done, after I had let him make his way into my heart and into my very blood, that I found this out. I saw his picture in a paper Roger Lavergne sent me. This show-girl's real name was Candace Pryor. He loved her. It was to her he called that night at the White Roe."

"Armande!" His voice was hushed, thick. "You knew of this, and you said nothing, did nothing — !"

"What would you have me do, Marc?" she demanded dejectedly. "Oh, I have gone over all this a thousand times. Is it for me, who accepted his love and thought it something sent straight from God, to turn upon him and betray him? I know that to you, to all right thinking people, it must seem monstrous, ugly, inhuman — what I have done. He killed Leon. He ran away. He came here — of all places. But that he should seek my love, the love of one whose brother — Help me, Marc."

He came over to her, took her hands in his. "I can help you there. I could have helped you long ago and would have, if I could even have dreamed of what you must have suffered. Loving him, letting him make love to you, thinking all the while that his heart was black — "

"No! No, I never thought that, but I could not understand. Why did he not confess to me, tell me the

THREE WHO LOVED HER

truth? How could he meet me, night after night, talk to me, look straight in my eyes, tell me he loved me — and harbor that ghastly thing in his heart. He might be innocent of the crime. Even so, why did he not speak?"

"He does not know."

Armande's hands went limp in his; she looked at him, incredulous, utterly puzzled.

"He does not know? What do you mean? How could he —"

"No memory," said Marc. "Only a fog in his mind; only grayness — all that happened before that night we found him — only darkness, in which, he told me, lurked something so ugly that he prayed to God he would not ever remember it again. It was she, this girl Candace. He must have cared very much; he must have believed in her — believed terribly."

"You have brought me some happiness, Marc. You have let some light into my heart. He did not know. I see now. Often I wondered at the strange things he said — that he had no one, no place to go to, that here he could have peace. Peace — there can be no peace for him! But why did he not confide in me?"

"He was happy just to be with you. He asked me to keep quiet, to tell no one. He wanted no pity, no notoriety. I think he feared his past and would have been glad if it were never made known to him."

"Perhaps," said Armande, "he was right at that. Would it not be better if he never knew? Suppose he did do it, Marc?"

"There is the law, you know."

"You mean they would take him and put him to death?"

"If he were shown to be guilty."

She drew her hands from Marc's. "No. No, they can't do that. He mustn't know, Marc! You — you wouldn't tell on him. You wouldn't do that."

"What am I to do? What can I do? It is my duty, any man's duty. He is wanted — a fugitive. Why should I keep silent about him?"

"Because I ask you, Marc."

"You do not know what you ask. I love you — yes, I must say it. I have given all my life to loving you.

THREE WHO LOVED HER

Now you ask me to keep my mouth shut and let a murderer — "

"He is not! Do not say that!" His anger melted before her distress. He shrugged. "You ask a lot, Armande. What good can this do you? Or how will it benefit him — beyond saving his neck?"

"Do not give him up, Marc," she pleaded. "Let him go away in peace. He will go away."

"Why are you so sure he will go away?"

"Because he thinks there is nothing here for him any more. It may be as you say — he is afraid of the past; still more is he uncertain of the future. There is no light behind him; none ahead. I think for a while he had his dreams — of a Utopia — "

"There is none."

"More is the pity. Anyway, he has lost faith in his. Perhaps — I do not know — he has lost faith in me. But what can I do? I cannot tell him the truth; knowing the truth I cannot be with him. It is cruel, Marc. The day I got the paper from Roger and read the ugly story, and saw him there, his picture, my blood boiled, then froze; my life seemed as if it would end, and I did not care. I did not care, Marc! "

He put his hand upon her shoulder, patted it lightly. "Don't take it so hard, Armande. One will do all that lies in one's power. I shall not give him away, but it is only a matter of time before someone else sees him and recognizes him."

"Then we must get him to go away."

"Where can he go? No place would be safe for him; in fact, he is less likely to be discovered here than elsewhere, but discovered he will be, and should it become known that you and I kept our mouths closed —"

"I know." She nodded. "People will think the worst and say it — they'll say I shielded him because he was my lover, they'll say I'm inhuman — they'll want to bait the witch."

"They will not like it." Marc's face was very grave. "As you say, they will interpret it all in the worst way possible; they'll say you shielded a criminal, care more for him than for the fact that he'd killed your brother."

"Don't, Marc. When you put it like that, it all seems terrible; it seems ugly and vile. And it isn't really. I know it isn't. There was something fine and good about

THREE WHO LOVED HER

our friendship, something beautiful about it all. I couldn't hate him for I'd learned to love him. Even — even if he were guilty I could not hate him. But he's not. He couldn't be."

"It seems quite clear that he not only could be guilty, but is. Your faith in him is a lovely thing, Armande."

"It is all I have, all I can cling to. So desperately I cling to it, Marc; and I won't give it up. From the first moment I saw this man I believed in him. I'll go on believing."

"Yes." Marc shrugged ruefully. "It is safe to say you will. And such faith as yours must be a help to any man. But you are rash to side with him, to come forth as his protector."

"Rash! I merely act as my heart tells me to act. It must be right. Say you think it's right."

"I can't say that, Armande. But right or wrong, I want you to know that I am with you. I'd go down into hell for you. They'll say you've put a spell, a witching on me too. And you have — a lovely spell."

"Kind Marc!" She stroked his hair, held his arm

as they walked to the door.

"Goodnight, Armande." He pressed her hand briefly and hurried down to his car. Roger, Marc, John Gower, who was Michael Dumont, she had sped them all on their way this winter night — two of them might never again return to her and her heart grew leaden at the thought. But Marc would always be there, Marc would always come to her, loving her so much, asking of her so little —

"He makes me feel small, selfish and unworthy." She went slowly upstairs to her room, touching softly in benediction the knob of Paul Emil's door as she passed.

CHAPTER IX

AT THE WHITE ROE

THE gray of a winter dusk seeped through the grimy windows of the little printing-shop of Alphonse Trudel, which is on the straggling main street of St. Bruno village, sandwiched between Comeau's garage and the dry-goods store of Edmond Cormier. Smudged paper, broken type and scattered bits of the multiplex paraphernalia used in the art of printing, littered the little place with its antique hand-press that, so ancient was it, seemed as if old Caxton himself had left it behind him and his ghost might come back any night to knock off a spirit-edition of " The Game and Playe of Chesse."

But John Gower, he they called *l'Etranger*, the dark and silent young man who lived at the White Roe, worked at the antique contraption today, knocking out smudgy posters announcing that a meeting of the rate-

FOG OVER FUNDY

payers of St. Bruno Ouest would be held early in December at the parish-hall to consider the matter of snow-removal.

"And a pretty serious matter for consideration," mused John Gower, A.B., gazing out at the banks piled higher than his head, in the village street; at the countless tiny feathers that fell, fell, silently, monotonously, covering the marsh-lands deeper and ever deeper. " Another day of this and one might as well abandon the idea of getting away before Spring. Away — " He shook his head wearily — " I don't want to go away, but I can't linger here. Maybe it will be the same every place I go." He grinned a rueful grin at the fancy. " Maybe if I went to the newspapers and told them my story they'd spread it all around and I'd find out who I was. No! "

He said the " No! " so vehemently that old Trudel, looming, stripe-aproned in the gloomy doorway of the storeroom, jumped like a rabbit and peered nervously over his rimless glasses to see whom the Stranger talked to. No one. There was no one. The old fellow's heart fluttered. He regretted, almost, the day he had engaged this odd young man. Of course, at that time, being a

AT THE WHITE ROE

confirmed bachelor and teetotaler and a bit of an unbeliever, which things automatically shut him off pretty well from St. Bruno society, he had heard little of John Gower. Then, too, John Gower wasn't the easiest person to say no to. He had a pleasant, open, cheerful way about him. He looked, the old printer thought that day, like a man whose troubles are few and those taken lightly. He was strong and willing.

Then had come, filtering through to Trudel's furry ears, as the light to his shop through the dust-caked windows, all the village gossip about his new apprentice — about his roaming over the moors by night, of his meeting that strange girl, reputedly a witch, Armande de Vysart, in the church by moonlight, of his holding converse with invisible presences. And Trudel, for all his bit of unbelief, was not by any means free of the ancient taint of superstition that is in all the marsh-dwellers. As he made his way slowly over to his little desk against the wall by the window he looked apprehensively about him as if expecting the devil to nudge him at any step or a black cat to leap up on his shoulder and bite his ear.

FOG OVER FUNDY

But there was nothing like that. The Stranger bent busily to his work. He was quick and smart and happy at his task, Trudel admitted, peering over his shoulder at the keen, dark profile, the wavy hair, the silent and eager eyes. Seemed to look right through you, those eyes — to have a life of their own, burning, vivid, strong. Who and what was he? Not a sailor, to be sure; nor yet a printer, though in a short time he would be. Something very queer about him. And he would not talk. Never a word of any event in his life before he came to St. Bruno. It was as if he had only then come upon the earth.

" Do you not find this a dull place, M'sieur Gower? " piped the old man, speaking casually, feigning to be very busy with a bundle of galleys, not a word of which was registering upon his brain. " For a man like you, now, who must have been to many foreign lands and seen places strange and fascinating, there is nothing that I can see to commend this bleak and barren world." He gestured with a dry, veined hand. " Nothing here to make your life worthwhile."

John Gower smiled, brushed a nervous hand over his

AT THE WHITE ROE

brow, over his glossy hair — a quick, instinctive gesture. So often had old Trudel seen him do just that, then look intently into nothingness. He drew a deep breath. "There is as much here, I fancy, as any place else. What does a man need? Food to eat, a place to sleep in, freedom to come and go, one to love — "

"You have found those things, m'sieur!"

"I have found them. For the first time in my life — of that I am sure — I found them all, and I was happy. I found them, my friend, and in the joy of finding and knowing them, I forgot that it is one thing to get; another to keep. So many considerations enter into it. Of these, in the first bliss, I took no count. Then they forced themselves upon me. Life will never let one live. A paradox, is it not?"

Trudel rubbed his bony lantern-jaw and shook his head sagely, though, not for the life of him could he grasp what the stranger was talking about. He hazarded a shot in the dark: "Then you will not be staying here?"

John Gower wiped his hands on his apron deliberately and walked to the sink in the corner. "I shall not be staying long, I think."

"Where then will you go?"

"Ah, there you have me. Where indeed!"

"But your home, your friends — !"

"I must find them, I suppose."

"One would think — " The printer laughed hollowly, "that your home and friends were things you had to search for in the dark."

The Stranger, his hands covered with soapsuds, turned to grin merrily at Trudel. "One would think so, eh?" He laughed. "Things to search for in the dark."

He finished his washing up and put on his warm coat and cap. Lights were blinking out through the snow along the village street. A sleigh passed with a merry jangling of bells. Old Trudel poked at the stove. John Gower gave him goodnight, said he would be on hand early to help with the posters for a séance that was being given shortly by *Le cercle Acadien de la jeunesse Canadienne*, and stepped out into the snow.

He loved it — the icy bite of the north-east wind, the soft sting of snow-flakes against his cheek. After

AT THE WHITE ROE

the stuffiness of the printery, which Trudel, being old and thin-blooded, kept at fever heat, it was like plunging from the blistering sun into a pool of blessed chill. John Gower walked with long, forceful strides, looking pleasantly at the glowing window-panes of the cottages, where boughs and sprigs of fir and spruce were laid on the sill between the outer and inner sashes, behind which moved the wholesome, happy existence of the Acadians.

He envied them their peace, the fullness of their lives, the quiet joys and freedom from cares and alarms. Yes, one could live here and count the world well lost. He had thought nothing could be better than to linger in this spot. Here were sunsets and dawns, quiet mirth and blessed calm. And when she had come into his life, when, that night of magic moonlight, her witch-music had stolen into his heart and possessed it, he had felt that nothing in this world could be comparable with the joy he knew, let alone surpass it.

But there were so many things, in her life and his. She could never marry him in his condition of printer's apprentice. Thinking of the wage he earned, he smiled,

FOG OVER FUNDY

and wondered if the exchequer would stand the purchase of a fresh packet of pipe-tobacco. And how, anyway, could he dare to love her, let alone think of making her his own. A nobody — less than a nobody. John Gower, A.B. of Far Rockaway, New York. He had written to Far Rockaway, asking information about John Gower. No one there, it seemed, knew anything at all about such a person. He had the town-clerk's letter in his pocket. Somehow it hadn't depressed him, that letter. When he read it there was relief in his heart and it was with joy rather than with doubt or perplexity that he folded it up and put it away. Someday he would know who he was and what? But did he want to know?

Sometimes he felt — felt most surely — that far out upon the gray sea that was his past, dark ships sailed — ships that it would not be good to board again; that in the depths of that gray sea lurked monsters ugly and uncouth. Here, upon the shore of the present, he was safe, he could be happy. What if, out of that past, were it restored to him, should come something that would destroy the quiet wonder that now dwelt in his heart? What if things should reach out of it like evil tentacles

AT THE WHITE ROE

to draw him back into something he did not ever regret nor often seek to know?

Well, best not to think of it now. No good to think of it. Life was good. The snow was good, and the winter night. At the White Roe there would be a great fire roaring on the hearth in the snug parlor; a warm supper awaiting him, a room to rest in, books to read, a pipe to smoke and dreams to dream. He bought his tobacco, strong, coarse Canadian leaf, so vile that, once smoked, a man can smoke no other, his sense of taste having been destroyed at the first puff. But it was lovelier than Latakia and richer than Perique to John Gower as he loaded his pipe, lighted and inverted it and trudged off along the street to the inn by the crossroads.

The windows of the White Roe shone warmly, cheerfully, through the driving snow, and the battered signboard swung groaningly in the gusts. John Gower kicked the snow from his boots and brushed it from his trouser-legs with the broom left on the porch for that purpose. Within, the fireside-circle had not yet assembled. Two commercial-travellers, snow-bound, were sitting at the table in the dining-room off the parlour

FOG OVER FUNDY

and Elodie, in spic white apron and cap, was carrying a steaming tray into them. John Gower warmed his hands at the fireside and readily agreed with Isaac Proux, who had followed Elodie through the swinging-door of the kitchen, that it was a great storm and promised to be a bitter night.

" But it will clear, m'sieur, before midnight, if I mistake not, and set in colder than ever."

" A good night to be indoors, M'sieur Proux."

" God pity all wayfarers and men at sea," said Isaac fervently. " Tonight there is roast-beef with turnips and potatoes, black pudding and lemon-pie."

" Amen," said John Gower, and went up to his room.

One of the commercial-travellers, a fat fellow named Ben Gallant, got up from the table and walked over to Isaac, busy piling fresh logs on the fire and mentally grumbling at the amount of fuel one required on these cruelly cold nights. The traveller touched Isaac's shoulder. The landlord straightened up and stared with his one hollow eye.

" Yes, m'sieur? The roast is overdone, no? The pudding — "

AT THE WHITE ROE

"That man?" A fat thumb jerked towards the stairs. "Who is he?"

Isaac shrugged. "His name is John Gower. He alone survived from the wreck of the yacht Triton which occurred last fall. Now he works at the printery of Alphonse Trudel in St. Bruno."

Ben Gallant's moon face was creased in puzzlement. "Strange," he said. "Very strange! I've seen that face. Seen it — " He drew in his lips, shook his bald head impatiently. "I can't think where. But I glanced up from the table as he was talking to you and it came to me in a flash. 'I've seen that fellow before,' I said. Couldn't forget that face. Looks like March, the movie-actor. A sailor, you say he was?"

"A.B.," nodded Isaac. "Able-bodied seaman."

"Well — " Ben turned back to his second helping of roast beef, determined to dawdle over it until John Gower should come to his dinner. He was a persistent fellow, Ben. He had once spent forty dollars and fifty cents on a course of memory-training which guaranteed that those who took it would never forget a face. It piqued him to think that here was a man he should know

FOG OVER FUNDY

and did know, yet could not place, even by applying five dollars' worth of post-graduate lessons.

John Gower came downstairs presently and took the chair opposite Ben, with a pleasant good evening for him and the other traveller, a dyspeptic-looking individual named Page, who sold patent-medicines.

"American, eh?" said Ben. "I could tell that the first word you said."

John Gower's brows went up a trifle. He thanked Elodie for his plate of vegetable-soup, broke a roll, and took a mouthful of soup before he said, "Now that is odd — very odd indeed."

"Why?" Ben was not easily abashed. "What is odd about it?"

"I couldn't tell, myself," smiled John Gower. "So it's odd, now isn't it? — that a stranger like you could get it so quickly."

"You didn't know yourself!" Ben put down a forkful of roast-beef, turnip and potato. "How d'you mean?"

"I thought I made myself clear. Maybe I didn't. Well, suppose I am an American?"

AT THE WHITE ROE

"Mm." Ben went through the frowning and head-shaking. The course was falling-down on him. "You'll pardon me, Mr. Gower, isn't it — ?"

"Gower."

"— but I'm sure I've seen you before."

"Is that so? Do you know, I rather hope you have? Where was it you saw me?"

"That I can't say. Your face is familiar — so darned familiar that I felt I ought to know you the moment I set eyes on you."

"Well —" John Gower applied himself to his dinner. "Maybe you will recall presently where it was you saw me. I'd help you — be most pleased to, in fact — but the truth is I'm in just the same predicament you are. I mean I don't know where it was that you think you should have seen me."

"No. Well —" Ben took a final look at that dark, lively visage, and, for the time, gave it up. "Maybe I was mistaken. Maybe it's that you resemble someone closely — someone I know very well."

"Probably that's it," agreed John Gower, relieved, though for a moment he had hoped that here, so unex-

FOG OVER FUNDY

pectedly, from this pudgy fellow, he was going to learn something that might make or unmake his life to come.

By the time the coffee was served, the evening habitues were beginning to gather. They came in, noses red with the cold, beards glistening with snow, and flocked to the fire, seeking to thaw the chill from their ancient bones. Jean Belliveau and Floribert Gaudet, huge gray-bearded old fellows, like Erlkings from some awful, frozen forest came first; Martin Theriault followed them; then came Hormidas Breau, the cobbler, and four huge louts of countrymen, the brothers Malenfant, and a half dozen others, among them Monsieur Léandre Frechette, local newspaper-correspondent, poet and littérateur.

Léandre, with his bobbed tow-coloured hair and outstuck Adam's apple, did not often honour the White Roe with his presence; had scarcely visited it at all in fact until John Gower had come there. Now, every week or so, he would drop in of an evening and take a seat by the fire, dispensing bits of classical knowledge and malapropos gems of verse and taking placidly, in

AT THE WHITE ROE

return, the open-mouthed awe of the great-booted rustics.

With John Gower, whom he considered a man worthy of his steel, the elongated poet was eager to talk. He had a romantic imagination, had Léandre Frechette, and a flair for the unusual and mysterious. But, for all his horse-faced pleasantness, he had not got very far with the Stranger. John Gower, in fact, looked upon him as something of an oddity and found his ponderous English periods and quotation-laden speech by turns amusing and dull.

Tonight, though, John Gower felt himself in a mood for company, even that of this Ichabod Crane of the marshes. He smiled pleasantly as he came from the dining-room, and stopped by the little table where Léandre was sitting, to fill his pipe and light it.

"A pleasant night indoors, M'sieur Frechette," he remarked, looking down at Léandre over the flame of the match, wondering if this local genius ever changed his high stiff collar or undid the greasy polka-dot bowtie that circled his neck so like a turkey-gobbler's.

"A night," rumbled Léandre, lifting his chin most

FOG OVER FUNDY

theatrically, " for the worship of the Lares and Penates, M'sieur Gower — a night on which the genial warmth of the fire seems to penetrate most — most deeply into our hearts — seems even to let into the deep, dark caverns of our hearts some of its ruddy and generous light."

" Quite," agreed the Stranger, tamping down the tobacco in his pipe. " How about a game of checkers? "

" Gladly," assented Léandre, " will I match my skill with yours. Be seated."

There was an inlaid draughts-board on the table, and from its drawer Léandre produced the well-used checkers, and they set about their play.

In the warm air tobacco-smoke floated in gray-blue, pungent wreaths, the ruddy glow of the fire merged with the light of shaded lamps; the logs crackled, there was the hum of deep voices discussing cattle and the scarcity of feed and the vigor of the winter and the prospects of spring. The radio, long out of repair, but functioning again after the ministrations of an itinerant mechanic, who had worked on it that morning for his dinner, played a medley of French-Canadian folk-songs

AT THE WHITE ROE

broadcast from Montreal, and not, the critical audience agreed, half so good to listen to nor quarter so well sung as those heard in this very parlour on many a night like this.

John Gower's fingers tapped on the table to the rollicking rhythm —

>Trois gros canards s'en vont baignant
>En roulant me boule.
>Rouli-roulant me boulie roulant
>En roulant me boule.

And the great clogs and shoepacks of the rustics beat time. Outside, the wind abated, the snow tapped lighter against the window panes and finally ceased. Isaac went to the door and looked out. " It is clear," he announced. " And bitter cold and a full moon rising. What a night, *mes amis* — what a wondrous night! "

A full moon rising.

Curious, cautious eyes glanced at the dark Stranger, intent upon the manoeuvering of a red king pressed hard by two of Léandre's black ones. They saw him forget,

FOG OVER FUNDY

for a moment, the game he played, and stare at the windows, at the blue-silver brightness flooding over the marshlands and the sea. And they thought, " The Moon Witch calls tonight. Soon will come the strains of unholy music from the church. Soon he will go to her."

He finished his game, making short shrift of Léandre's cunning. He rose. " It has been most enjoyable, M'sieur Frechette, and thank you for the opportunity of playing with you. I think now I shall go for a walk."

He went up to his room and came down shortly, dressed for the frosty night. He walked through a deep, pregnant silence. Eyes stared fixedly at the fire; minds focussed upon a single theme — the Stranger and the Witch and the round pale moon. How long could this go on? How long before still greater evil came of it than what already had come — the murder of Léon de Vysart, the passing of Suzanne, the departure of Ulric, the taking of Paul Emil Delagarde to live in the great lonely house with the strange girl who, they were sure, was no fit guardian for the child; more, who had done evil to the child's mother in order to get him.

AT THE WHITE ROE

"He goes to her," muttered Hormidas Breau, the cobbler, when the inn-door closed upon John Gower's broad back. "Nights like this are made for such as those two. I tell you it is not right. It is a scandal."

"Maybe it is love," put in Isaac philosophically.

"Love — between that Dark One and her!" Hormidas scoffed. "A queer love! Why should they meet on such a night as this unless to hatch some more evil? Ruin began for that house when the Stranger came out of the sea. Between him and her they've fixed to destroy it and possess it. She will have him. Anything she wants she can have. She got her brothers out of the way. Who knows but what big Ulric is dead by now? She brought death to Suzanne Delagarde and stole the boy. She will bring evil to us all. These were all evil things."

The others nodded. "What has this Stranger, who pretends to be a printer, to do with one who is supposed to be a great lady?" demanded Hormidas. "Not likely she'd refuse the other men who wanted her, in favor of this one — unless there's something we don't know. They belong to the devil, the both of them, if you ask me."

FOG OVER FUNDY

"*Assez!*" Isaac scowled and glared with his good eye. " He seems quiet and decent enough, this Stranger. What is there that is so evil about it, Hormidas? They are young. They are in love, no doubt."

" Bah! " The cobbler spat into the hearth and shook his grizzled head. " You can't tell me that. You can't tell any of us that. We've talked about it enough. This fellow came out of the sea from nowhere, and he should be thrown back into the sea."

" That's right! " Godfroi, the eldest of the four Malenfants, cut-in. " Throw him into the sea." His dark brothers nodded assent. Of late, they had lost by seizure a goodly number of kegs of contraband rum, in which they did a thriving trade. In one of the seizures, Michel Pettigrew, a kinsman of theirs, had been shot. It was obvious that the Mounties had been tipped-off about the landing of the cargoes and their stupid minds fixed upon the Stranger as having given the information. Was he not forever wandering about the marshes at night? Hadn't they seen him in coves and inlets where he had no business to be? In league with the devil or in league

AT THE WHITE ROE

with the R. C. M. P., it didn't matter to them. They didn't like him.

" But you can't condemn a man like that," persisted Isaac, who was a pretty fair-minded man and objected to losing a good customer like John Gower. " He hasn't done anything you can really call wrong. Hasn't broken any laws that I know of."

Stony silence greeted Isaac's defence. The peasant-mind fears and distrusts the Unknown: that was why there were none there save Isaac to say a word in defence of Armande de Vysart or the Stranger. Nothing so dark, nothing so occult or evil that either of those two could not be suspected of it and when the twain were united none could conjecture what pestilences and calamities might fall upon the community.

"No good can come of it," croaked Hormidas. " Mark me, it's a dark and cruel business they're about."

John Gower, perhaps not entirely unaware of the nature of the discussion he had left behind him, walked briskly along the snow-road to St. Bruno. No room however bright and warm, no company however genial and good, could keep him in on a night like this. Had he always, he wondered, reacted in just this way? Had he wanted always to run into the peace and wonder of the night, to steep his soul in its beauty, to feel something sublime reaching out of him, seeking the perfection of beauty that seemed at this time to be nearest of attainment? Was it mostly for her that he went? His heart hungered for her; his eyes for her eyes, his lips for her lips. Yet he did not know that she would come to him. It would be only Fate's doings if they met. Perhaps she would be at the church tonight, playing those wild, plaintive harmonies that filled his soul with awe; perhaps, regretting other nights, she would not come now; and perhaps it was better so.

In front of Dr. Marc Duclos' cottage, the Stranger hesitated. The lights in Marc's study burned bright. He liked Marc, liked him more because he knew of the young medico's long devotion to Armande de Vysart. And Marc had been most kind to him. Marc had told him he would one day remember his past, that it might come back to him by degrees, might come flooding all

AT THE WHITE ROE

at once like bright light into the darkness of his mind. Too, Marc had understood his willingness to let that past go, to take the present gladly, for what it had to offer.

John Gower walked up the path to the door and rang the bell. Marc's housekeeper came. Yes, the doctor was in. He was upstairs but would be down in a moment. Would monsieur enter.

She ushered him into Marc's cosy room — a room that made John Gower sigh, with its shelves of books, its pictures and mementos of college days, its worn leather chairs, its pipes and bric-a-brac — all the heterogeneous things that man, left by woman to his own devices, will gather unto himself. The Stranger sat in a chair by the hearth and looked shyly about him. Yes, it was a good room; from it you could draw a picture of him who dwelt in it.

And he loved her, this serious, brilliant young doctor. Hearing him speak of her, John Gower had known in an instant what she had meant and continued to mean in his life. Love and devotion the Stranger saw in Marc's eager, tired eyes — love that is unquestioning,

FOG OVER FUNDY

devotion that asks nothing in return. Why was it that she could not love Duclos? Why was it she could in an instant turn her back upon his life's loyalty and give the fresh wonder of her love to a nobody, a wanderer? The Stranger pressed his knuckles to his temples. It wasn't right. Nothing was right. He would go away at once — oh, anywhere, anywhere. He would tell Duclos tonight.

Restlessly he got up and wandered about the room, glancing idly at books and papers. Suddenly a paper crackled, almost torn apart with the sudden tightening of his grip upon it. A wild, terrible look sprang into his eyes. The paper shook with the aguish trembling of his hands. His breath came hard, loud there in the quiet room above the hissing of the fire.

"God!" he said in a whisper. "Oh, God — my God!"

Slowly he folded the paper, put it back where he had found it. He picked it up again, looked at the date-line. He closed his eyes and stood, tense, hands clenched, arms straight down at his sides, his face lifted, masque-like, as if yielding himself to Fate's bludgeoning, taking

AT THE WHITE ROE

it grandly, bearing it without flinching.

When Marc came in, he was sitting in the chair by the fireside. He stood up. He took Marc's hand hesitantly. " I — I was passing. I just dropped in."

" That is good. Sit down."

" No — no, I think I will stand, thank you. I came to tell you I'm going away from here — going away."

" Yes." Marc stared at the fire. " Going away, my friend. And still — " Marc tapped his brow — " nothing, *hein?* "

" Nothing — " John Gower smiled grimly. " Nothing, doctor — I may go to the death-chair — with nothing — here." He touched his brow.

" What! " Marc jerked erect, stared at him. " What do you mean? "

" You know what I mean. You know my name. You've known it for some time. You know what I've done — what I'm wanted for. A murderer — " He stared at his hands. " Blood on those hands — her brother's — and those hands — " His face contorted with a sudden access of fury, he took a step towards Marc. " Why didn't you tell me? Why'd you let me

FOG OVER FUNDY

walk in this fool's paradise? Why'd you do a rotten thing like that?"

Marc looked at him calmly. "She asked me to."

The Stranger's hands dropped. Incredulous, bewildered, his eyes probed into Marc's. "She — she knew — !"

"Long before I did. She knew — shortly after she —"

"After that night. She must have found it out after that night. That was why she avoided me. Yet when I came to her she — Tell me, doctor, did she know that I — I — that it was all black to me, that I did not — ?"

"She didn't know. She went through some hell, m'sieur, wondering if you who loved her had done this hideous thing —"

"She believes I did it then?"

"No. She does not believe — not for a moment. Do you?"

"I read of it there — in the paper. It reads as if I — I murdered this man in a fight over a — well, a woman who wasn't much."

"Candace," said Marc quietly. "Candace Pryor.

AT THE WHITE ROE

You called her name the night you came to the White Roe."

"Candace!" whispered the Stranger. "I seem to — No! No, I cannot recall. I cannot. What am I to do? What can I do? They can't condemn me for a crime I don't know about!"

"If you did it —"

"I might have done it. I might have. All the time I've known there was something ugly back there, something vile and slimy. Maybe that's why I was willing to let the past go; maybe that's why I found the present so worthwhile; maybe I wanted to stay here because here was peace and goodness."

"It could be," said Marc. "But you cannot stay here now. You would not."

"No." He picked up his cap from the table, held it in his two hands and stared at it, a queer, tired, unhappy twist to his mouth. "I'll go all right. She knows I —"

"She knows that towards her you acted in good faith. She begged me, when I told her of my discovery, to shield you, as she has done."

"Yes. Yes, she shielded me. She — she loved me,

FOG OVER FUNDY

and I loved her. It seemed so good, so like heaven; I walked on the clouds; I was a god. Now this — life can't do this to me — " His voice was bewildered, almost querulous. " It can't do a rotten thing like this. It can't give me her and give me the memory of her and then tell me suddenly I'm a felon, a beast, a murderer; that I killed the brother she loved. It cannot do that! "

Marc felt a stab in his own breast. The man was strong, but what man was strong enough to have his soul torn and twisted, racked and tortured like this? " Don't despair," he said kindly. " It may come back to you. It may not be so bad — "

" But what am I to do? What can I do? If I give myself up, who will believe me? Who but will think, as all this time they've been thinking, that I was guilty, that I ran away, that I stayed hidden here — " He looked wildly about him. " I must go. I must get out. I can't stay. Thank you. Thank her — "

He hurried to the door. Marc called to him. He did not answer. Marc ran after him and caught his arm, but he flung Marc away and ran down the path to the road

AT THE WHITE ROE

like one the devil was chasing.

"No use to run," muttered Marc. "No use at all. It will catch up with him one day — God help him."

In the parlor of the White Roe the rustics still circled the fire. Léandre Frechette played checkers with Ben Gallant, disdainfully, for he considered the traveller a very uncouth person indeed, a man on whom were wasted utterly the choice pearls from Racine, Fénelon and Bossuet, that trickled from his lips. The villagers still talked of the Stranger, of Armande de Vysart, of Leon and Ulric and the others of the family they had known. The radio tinkled out the incongruous strains of jazz played by a sleek-haired band of musicians in some great far-distant hotel. Then came the announcement of a news-broadcast, and the conversation halted.

From the great world outside, words flowed into the warm cosy inn-parlour — words like invisible antennae, reaching there, taking hold, fastening, as if for this one spot they had been forever destined. A smooth voice speaking — the name of Leon de Vysart — Chairs

FOG OVER FUNDY

scraped on the floor, a pipe bowl that had been tapping hollowly against a fire-dog was drawn away — "Michael Dumont, wealthy, socially prominent, missing since the time de Vysart was found shot to death in Dumont's lonely hunting-lodge in the Adirondacks. Search for Dumont has proved fruitless. A handsome man, young, dark hair, dark eyes, a small white cross-shaped scar on his right wrist — "

"Great God!" Léandre Frechette's hand flew from the man he had been moving and sent the rest of the checkers flying on the floor. He sprang to his feet, his chair went crashing. The others stood up as hastily, mouths agape. The radio's voice was lost. Léandre's hand tore at his collar as if to loose it to give himself breath. His fishy eyes protruded and his hands waved like the sails of a windmill.

"Messieurs!" he gasped. "It — " His hands beat the air as if by their motion he would force himself to bring forth the words — "It is he — this man we know as John Gower — the murderer — I saw that little scar like a cross all evening as we played. It burned into my mind."

AT THE WHITE ROE

"That's it!" Ben Gallant said triumphantly. "I knew it. I've seen his picture. He's the man. The murderer!"

They stared at one another in silence. How clear it all was now, his staying here in this lost village on the world's edge, his silence, his strange doings.

"And it is she —" Hormidas Breau's voice was husky with horror — "Leon's own sister — who consorts with this man. It is monstrous! It is horrible!"

"She may not — know," muttered Isaac.

"She knows! She knows! She is a witch. She —"

"Even now," said another, "they are together — maybe in God's house — this murderer — and did she not put the Evil Eye on Suzanne Delagarde!"

"Come!" Godfroi Malenfant and his brothers led the crowd that poured out of the White Roe; the old men trudged along in the rear. Only Isaac stayed by the fire, going back there after they had all gone, like fantastic creatures with more fantastic shadows dancing grotesque on the snow like a shadow-army beside them. Isaac did not go. He sat by his fire and thought of her —

FOG OVER FUNDY

so tall, so white, so ashen-blonde of hair and blue of eye; of the dark stranger held tenderly in her arms while brandy was poured into his sea-cold lips. And, as on that other night, Isaac crossed himself piously.

CHAPTER X

LIGHT WHERE WAS DARKNESS

FOR a while he hurried aimlessly along, stumbling, blind, in a wilderness of doubts and fears. The world, the hand of every man in it, was against him. He felt dwarfed, a pygmy, in the immensity of the night, a tiny speck crawling over infinities of space. Friendless, hunted, driven — and he was without power, he groped in blackness and his powerlessness to know the truth, the horrible possibility that the truth in all its fullness might never be made manifest to him, maddened and goaded his spirit until it seemed body and spirit must crack with the strain.

He slowed his stumbling pace as he passed beyond the village. Why hurry? You couldn't hurry away from a thing like this. It would pursue you ever, relentlessly, tirelessly; you couldn't hide from it or find rest from

FOG OVER FUNDY

it; you could never escape it. He wished fervently to God that, guilty or innocent of this awful thing, he had gone on in his blindness. He had enjoyed here for a little while a full measure of happiness; then it had been snatched cruelly from his hands. And there was nothing now for him; less than nothing. Was ever man, he wondered, in a predicament so grim, so terrible in its implications. A murderer! He was no murderer. He knew it. No, not he; not ever. That other man, that Dumont, that monster Hyde. Maybe he had done this thing. Yes, leering, mocking, sneering out of the gray blackness, he came forward and said to John Gower, to the hunted, cowering Henry Jekyll: " I might have done it. Sure, probably I did do it. Why not? You say you didn't do it; John Gower didn't do it — John Gower who found heaven in the eyes of the dead man's sister, who gave his fine heart to her, could never do a thing like that. Of course not! But tell that to the world who despises you for a cowardly murderer; tell it to the police who have been hunting you, who think you have been hiding from them. Tell them that John Gower is not responsible for the deeds of Michael Dumont. Tell them, and see

LIGHT WHERE WAS DARKNESS

what they do. They'll laugh! They'll laugh at you."

He stared up wild-eyed at the stars, at the serene majestic face of the moon. Dumont — he hated Dumont, hated everything about him. Let him feel his hands at Dumont's throat, let him destroy Dumont, throw him upon the earth and stamp upon his evil face. Let John Gower do this and let John Gower go on in peace, happy in his humble work, in his quiet room, in his reading, happy in being allowed to see her and love her. But the man Dumont, no less than the man John Gower, had had reality and though a different spirit might dwell in this body of his, it was he who must answer for the doings of both of them.

But she knew — Armande. She believed in him. No — no, it was in Dumont she believed. Michael Dumont did not do this thing. Could she not see that John Gower, who loved her, who adored her — that it was utterly impossible for him to have done it. John Gower had been born in her arms that night of storm; hers the first hand that had touched him. She must see it that way. She must believe, as he, that the other man was dead, that for her he had never lived —

FOG OVER FUNDY

Madness! He told himself bitterly it was madness. What did anyone care for what he thought. What would they say about his ideas other than that they were those of a crazy man. He'd have to stop thinking about it. He'd have to do something. He couldn't go tramping on forever through this frosty night of horror. Ugly the moon looked, cold and mocking — had he ever loved it, ever thought it beautiful! Cruel the stars looked, like menacing points ready to pierce him — what had he ever seen that was lovely about them! And the whole world an ugly, evil, fearsome place — nothing good, nothing worthwhile, nothing to be kind to him or to bring a tiny bit of gladness into his tormented heart —

Then he heard it. Light, plaintive, soft, sweet and clear upon the frosty stillness of the night. Music — music not of earth, like the strains of some heavenly symphony, filling all the air, drifting deliciously from afar, bringing peace and calm into his spirit, slowing the mad race of his emotions, stopping his aimless steps. There by the gray stone gateway of the church he stood and listened. Only himself and she who played, now, in all the world. She knew — she knew, and she did not

LIGHT WHERE WAS DARKNESS

hate him nor cower away from him. The music spoke of hope, of faith, of — even — happiness. Happiness — a wild hope flamed up in his heart. Couldn't there be happiness yet — for her and him? Couldn't Michael Dumont give happiness to John Gower — Dumont with his wealth? Money could do so many things — even with stern Justice. Money might buy his freedom — No, it would buy Dumont's freedom, but never John Gower's. No, let Dumont suffer, let him die.

"But Dumont is dead," he muttered. "Dead."

Slowly he walked up through the churchyard. Gravestones there, white stones, half buried in the whiter snow. And one of them marking the grave of Leon. Close to that grave he, John Gower, had taken her into his arms and held her and loved her. Sacrilege? Not for John Gower; but for Dumont, yes. He opened the door and went into the vestibule, stood at the foot of the winding stairs as he had stood that other night. Soon she would stop playing. She would come down the stairs. She would see him there. She would know in an instant what had happened to him, how a thunderbolt had been hurled into his life, a mighty rock into the glass house of flowers where he had thought to take up his abode.

He would go away, and she would not try to stay him. It was the end of this that had been so lovely; the end of everything. His icy hand gripped the newel-post hard when the music ceased. She would be coming now. He heard her light step on the landing above. He wanted to run now, to avoid her, to cower into the darkness of the stair-well so that she would not see him. He could not move. Helpless, abashed, dreading the moment of their meeting, yet praying for it, he waited there. He saw her now, a figure of light. Moon Witch they called her, but he, seeing her there in the long blue silver shafts of light, thought of her as the Madonna of the Moon, and he could have prayed to her, he could have flung himself upon his knees and, stretching out his arms supplicatingly, have said to her —

> "Tower of Ivory,
> Pray for me.
> House of Gold,
> Pray for me.
> Gate of Heaven, Morning Star,
> Pray for me."

LIGHT WHERE WAS DARKNESS

She stood on the bottom step, her eyes on a level with his. She did not speak, but on her lips was a smile, gentle, serene, wistful. And she held out her hand to him and with a sound like a sob he seized it in both his and pressed it hard against his cheek, against his eyes that ached tormentingly, pressed it with terrible force as if he would lay it against his very soul.

"You forgive me. You did forgive me. I did not know. You understand that I did not know. You understand that to me it is as if it were some other person, some person of another world whom they accuse of this crime. He must have done it; I did not — not I who loved you, who prayed to you, who adored you and everything about you. Say you know that and believe it."

"I believe." Her hand came up and touched his cheek, his hair, and rested upon his shoulder. "Not for a moment did I cease to believe, though at times it was hard. It was very hard. But I was right. I know now, if I never knew, I was right. Not you, not anyone who was ever you, *cher,* could have done this thing. I could never believe that. I could never."

FOG OVER FUNDY

His head was bowed. He lifted his face to hers. He spoke gently, all the urgency, the terrible turbulence gone from his speech, even as from his heart it had ebbed. "You have saved me from hell, Armande. I don't care now — what happens. Now that I know you believe — Once you told me I was fine and good. I took that to me and treasured it. I was fine and good. I should not ever have forgotten it. I am fine and good, Armande."

"You are! Oh, you are!"

She came into his arms and his cold cheek lay against hers and he felt the wet of tears upon her lashes; he felt the swift strong beat of her heart, the pulse of her splendid life, the wonder of her beauty. To hold her like this forever, to live like this, to die like this — to be parted from her never. Her cheek moved against his, their lips met and all the world was gone away — gone all but this that was of eternity —

Rudely they were awakened, rudely torn apart. Shouts and mutterings and savage thumping upon the heavy oak of the tower door. "Come out! Come out! Murderer and Witch! Out of the House of God!" Out-

LIGHT WHERE WAS DARKNESS

side it seemed as if the wild sea raged, surged up, flung itself against the door. A hideous, appalling sound bursting upon the ancient stillness, a fearsome, blood-chilling thing, as if it were a pack of beasts who raged there, fangs bared, jaws slavering, red maws agape — to tear and rend and devour.

His hand clutched hers. " Armande! " he whispered. " What can this be! What do they mean! Surely they are insane — "

" Yes! Yes! " Her voice was calm but urgent. " Insane — that is it! We must not be afraid of them. Why should we be afraid? We have done no wrong."

" I will go," he said. But quicker than his words, she had darted to the door, flung it open and walked out upon the stone step. He followed her, stood by her side. The mob gave back, glowering, leashed for a moment. Men and women there, a score and more of them, like creatures not of earth, milling there in the moonlight, eyes fixed with fanatic rage, bodies tense, predatory hands ready to seize and destroy. Like some scene out of the dark ages — the tall, slender figure of the de Vysart, her face strangely white in the moonglow, her dark eyes

FOG OVER FUNDY

bright, her proud chin lifted — the man beside her, uncomprehending but unafraid. These two on the steps of the gray stone church, its high cross dark against the sky — the cross that stands for love and mercy and forgiveness — and the wolfish pack, gripped, maddened by superstition, ready to destroy this man and woman for some sin they could not name.

"What would you have with us?" Armande's voice cut clear into the bitter air. "What folly is this!"

"What black sin is this, witch!" called a woman's voice from the crowd. "What do you do there in the sacred place with a murderer? You know he is a murderer. You know it!"

"She knows it! She knows it! Take her! Take him! Destroy them both! Send the evil things back into the pit they came from!"

Like jackals they advanced slowly to the steps. Some had sticks. Some were armed with jagged pieces of ice. One of these, flung violently, shattered itself like glass against the church wall by the door.

"Go back!" cried Armande. "Go back! You do not know what you are doing. You are misled. You are —"

LIGHT WHERE WAS DARKNESS

Voices drowned out her voice. Where was the curé? Was there no help anywhere? With their clubs they would beat her and him into insensibility, with their claws they would tear their flesh. They were mad, mad, mad. God, could such a thing be done in this day! Could such a horrible deed be perpetrated in the very shadow of the church! She prayed to the God she knew and loved. Chunks of ice rained around her and the man who stood silently defiant beside her.

Suddenly she knew he was not there. He dashed past her, flung himself, his lithe body, into the very midst of them. She saw his fists flailing, saw figures sprawl on the snow, heard shouts and curses and growls as from a pit of savage animals. Rough hands seized her, pulled her down into the maelstrom, buffeted her, tore at her garments. She was upon the ground and heavy boots trampled in the snow around her. They were killing him, she knew. They would kill her. She heard the sharp bark of a gun and hard, stern voices — another voice she knew, that brought gladness into her heart — Marc's.

She felt the press give way from around her. Saw

FOG OVER FUNDY

men and women hurled to right and left, and Marc, wide-eyed, panting, burst through and flung himself on his knees and caught her in his arms. He was sobbing with rage, with fear for her.

"I am all right," she gasped. "A few bruises maybe. But — " She got to her feet, Marc's arm supporting her. "What have they done to him? Where is he?" She saw his prone figure, a trooper standing above him. The wild mob was being driven into a corner of the churchyard by two others of the police-detachment.

"God forgive them for this night's work," said Marc through his teeth as he knelt down by the Stranger's side. "If they have not killed this innocent man it is not their fault. Come! We must get him to the presbytery." He and the trooper lifted the limp form of John Gower. They carried him to the presbytery. Armande followed. Weak and spent from the terrible ordeal, she yet had strength enough left to pound upon the door until the panic-stricken housekeeper came to open it. The good curé had been away, and it is doubtful if his presence would have deterred the ravening pack.

They carried him in, laid him on the sofa in Père

LIGHT WHERE WAS DARKNESS

Archambeault's study. Armande sank weakly down into the curé's chair. Marcelline, the housekeeper, urged by Marc to hasten, brought brandy and hot water and cloth for bandages. Marc worked feverishly, deftly. Armande, hands clasped, watched him with wonder in her eyes and love. With him now was no thought other than that of saving this man's life, of opening his eyes, of bringing something back into his bloody and battered face.

"It may take time," he muttered. "Time. What a pity this should be." He straightened after a while. He smiled reassuringly at Armande. "I think he will be all right. He took a terrible beating."

"He threw himself into the midst of them," said Armande. "He tried to fight them away from me. It was terrible, Marc. It was hideous — hideous — " She covered her face with her hands, her shoulders, her body trembled. Marc came to her and smoothed her hair. "I can't help it, Marc. I did not believe that people could be like that. They were not themselves. They were like wild beasts."

"Exactly," said Marc. "They let themselves act like

beasts. Well, like beasts they got many a boot and cuff for their pains, and a number of them will pay plenty for what they have done. The police have them all. I was at the other end of the village when I heard of this. I telephoned to Sackville. There were some troopers there and they got here just in time."

"How — how did they know about him?" She looked piteously at the Stranger lying there so still, so lifeless — sadder now to behold than on the night he had dragged his battered body from the sea.

"They got it over the radio at the White Roe. But the fools did not hear all the broadcast. That Frechette jumped up when they spoke of a man with a cross-shaped scar on his wrist and some traveller remembered seeing a picture. They could not hear the radio. They were too ready to go out and kill. Had they listened to the rest of it all would have been well."

"The rest of it?" She looked at him eagerly. "Tell me, Marc. Is he — ?"

"This Pryor woman — or Wayland, as she calls herself — was hurt, in danger of death, I guess, and cowardly people are most cowardly when death is in

LIGHT WHERE WAS DARKNESS

the offing. *Bien!* Anyway, she told the truth. Dumont was not there when Leon was killed. It was an accident. She was play-acting, threatening to kill herself after Dumont left. Leon didn't know her well enough to laugh at her. He tried to take the gun from her. It went off — *tout simplement cela!*"

Armande had listened breathlessly. A great peace, a great rejoicing and thankfulness to God for His mercies, was in her heart. Free — he would be free now of all the black and cankerous things that would have eaten into his very soul. He would not be afraid now to take her into his arms, to speak to her of his love. Always he would be hers.

"She was furious at him," went on Marc, bending again to his patient, giving him brandy, "after he found out she was no good. He had been engaged to her and he took her pretty seriously. It hurt him, for he had trusted her. Well, she wanted to get back at him. 'Hell hath no furies —' She tried to pin Leon's death on him. At that, she might have got away with it —"

"Oh, I am glad, Marc — so glad!"

He looked over his shoulder and smiled at her. "And

FOG OVER FUNDY

I am glad too, Armande, for your sake — as well as his."

" He will be all right, Marc? You are sure — ? "

" Quite sure. Now he is coming-to. He speaks." Armande came over and knelt beside Marc. The Stranger's lips moved. " Armande! " he whispered. " Armande! "

" I am here." She touched his hand. His eyes opened slowly. He stared at her and smiled. He tried to sit up.

" Easy there! " Marc made him stay where he was. " You're better the way you are. You went through a worse storm tonight, *mon ami,* than the one that brought you to our village — that you found so full of peace and tranquillity." Marc grinned. " How do you feel now, M'sieur Gower? "

" Terrible," he said cheerfully. " And I really know my name now. I had a pea-jacket belonging to a chap named Gower. He started out in the lifeboat with me. I can recall the whole thing now. I was all cut up over Candace. I boarded Dave Loring's yacht a few minutes before she sailed. Whatever the wreck knocked out of place, this night has put back again. And I didn't do

LIGHT WHERE WAS DARKNESS

it — " There was infinite relief in his voice. " I didn't — "

" We know," said Armande. " She has told the truth, your Candace. She was threatening suicide, Leon tried to take the gun. It was that news over the radio, or part of it, that started the trouble tonight."

" She owned up, eh? I am so glad. Too bad your brother believed her: she never would have killed herself. Now I am free — free of everything. And you believed in me, Armande. It is so good to know that."

Marc stood up, told his patient to take it easy, and strolled out of the room. Nothing more there for him now — nothing more than there ever had been or ever would be. He was brave, Marc; but not brave enough to smile. Still, for the years that had gone, for the years he had loved her, he had no regrets — no regrets, for those years had left with him memories ripe and colored, memories sweet and immortal, of sunsets and dawns, of rains and soft winds blowing, of gardens by moonlight and little villages nestling in the green valleys, of white churches and quiet tombstones bent beneath ancient willows, of dews silvery at dawn and the spiders' won-

FOG OVER FUNDY

drous web, of flaming maples in the autumn and roaring fires of beech in the stone hearth just as dusk settled upon the earth; of the ploughboy's whistle and the sheep-dog's bark, of the smell of the woods after rain, of burning forests in the summer-drought, of — oh, a thousand things, piquant, poignant, food for the soul and balm for the heart that is warm and open. For these things, he thanked God and through them worshipped Him and in his love of them prayed to Him.

The Stranger's eyes held Armande's. " Storms and tempests," he said, " seem to bring us closest together, Armande."

" Tonight, when you were awaking, it was my name you spoke. I was happy."

" It will be always your name upon my lips. Should I awaken in another world it would be for you I'd call. Always with you — I shall be always with you now, Armande. With you I minded nothing. Even tonight on the church steps with that ugly throng waiting to destroy us, it didn't seem to matter, for you were with me. The darkness I lived in wasn't darkness, for you were always there, a bright light to guide me."

LIGHT WHERE WAS DARKNESS

" You talk too much. You will weary yourself."

" And I must not. There is tomorrow — and tomorrow there will be so much to do. We will be married soon — we will go to New York — "

" To New York, I — "

" And return here to live." He smiled. " It is as dear to me, in spite of this night, as it is to you. Here, for the first time, I really loved, really knew what love was. Here we'll live together, you and I, and the little boy, and always when there is a moon, we shall remember — "

Armande smiled, and murmured, as an echo, " We shall remember."

FORMAC FICTION TREASURES Also in the Series

By Frances Gillmor
Thumbcap Weir
Gid Wyn and his fiancée, Debbie MacQuarrie, are counting on getting her father's fishing weir when they get married in the spring; but there is one villager, Tony Luti, who thinks it's his weir and that it has been stolen from him. Luti sets out to destroy the young couple's dreams and his hatred gets greater with the passing months until one day, under cover of fog, he and his son take revenge.
ISBN 10: 0-88780-645-7 ISBN 13: 978-0-88780-645-2

By Evelyn Eaton
Restless are the Sails
Paul de Morpain, a prisoner-of-war in New England, overhears a plan to send an expedition against the French fortress at Louisbourg. He knows he must do whatever he can to warn the governor. It is 1744 — a dangerous time to attempt a 500-mile journey by sea and overland along dangerous forest trails.
ISBN 10: 0-88780-603-1 ISBN 13: 978-0-88780-603-2

Quietly My Captain Waits
This historical romance, set during the years of French-English struggle in New France, draws two lovers out of the shadows of history — Louise de Freneuse, married and widowed twice, and Pierre de Bonaventure, Fleet Captain in the French navy. Their almost impossible relationship helps them endure the day-to-day struggle in the fated settlement of Port Royal.
ISBN 10: 0-88780-544-2 ISBN 13: 978-0-88780-544-8

The Sea is So Wide
In the summer of 1755, Barbe Comeau offers her Annapolis Valley home as overnight shelter to an English officer and his surly companion. The Comeaus are unaware of the plans to confiscate the Acadian farms and send them all into exile. A few weeks later, the treachery unfolds and they are sent to an unknown land as pawns in the Anglo-French conflict.
ISBN 10: 0-88780-573-6 ISBN 13: 978-0-88780-573-8

By W. Albert Hickman
The Sacrifice of the Shannon
In the heart of Frederick Ashburn, sea captain and sportsman, there glows a secret fire of love for young Gertrude MacMichael. But her interests lie with Ashburn's fellow adventurer, the dashing and slightly mysterious Dave Wilson. From their hometown of Caribou (real-life Pictou) all three set out on a perilous journey to the ice fields in the Gulf of St. Lawrence to save a ship and its precious cargo — Gertrude's father. In almost constant danger, Wilson is willing to risk everything to bring the ship and crew to safety.
ISBN 10: 0-88780-542-6 ISBN 13: 978-0-88780-542-4

By Alice Jones (Alix John)
The Night Hawk
Set in Halifax during the American Civil War, a wealthy Southerner — beautiful, poised, intelligent and divorced — poses as a refugee in Halifax while using her social success to work undercover. The conviviality of the town's social elite, especially the British garrison officers is more than just a diversion when there is a war to be won.
ISBN 10: 0-88780-538-8 ISBN 13: 978-0-88780-538-7

A Privateer's Fortune
When Gilbert Clinch discovers a very valuable painting and statue in his deceased grandfather's attic, he begins to uncover some of his ancestor's secrets, including a will that allows Clinch to become a wealthy man, while at the same time disinheriting his cousins. His grandfather's business as a privateer and slave trader helped him amass wealth, power and prestige. Clinch has secrets of his own, including a clandestine love affair. From Nova Scotia, to the art salons in Paris and finally the gentility of English country mansions, Clinch and his lover, Isabel Broderick, become entangled in a haunting legacy.
ISBN 10: 0-88780-572-8 ISBN 13: 978-0-88780-572-1

By Evelyn Richardson
Desired Haven
Mercy Nickerson's father returns from a voyage to the Caribbean with a young Irishman he has saved from a shipwreck. Mercy and Dan are

instantly attracted to one another. Rather than go to Boston, Dan decides to stay and turn his ambition to the fishery and ship supply. But his desired haven becomes a more dangerous place than he intended when he turns to smuggling and his wife turns against him.
ISBN 10: 0-88780-675-9 ISBN 13: 978-0-88780-675-9

No Small Tempest
Adria Redmond's life in a sea-faring community is marked by deception and deceit before a tragedy forces her to recognize what's important in her life.
ISBN 10: 0-88780-706-2 ISBN 13: 978-088780-706-0

By Charles G.D. Roberts
The Forge in the Forest: An Acadian Romance
Jean de Mer, an "Acadian Ranger," returns, after three years' absence, to his lands on the shores of Minas Basin to find his son Marc in trouble with the Black Abbé — a French partisan leader. Marc is waiting to be tried as a spy. Together father and son make a daring escape but Marc is wounded and Jean must endure a perilous canoe journey with a young English woman to rescue her child from the Black Abbé.
ISBN 10: 0-88780-604-X ISBN 13: 978-0-88780-604-9

The Heart That Knows
She was abandoned just hours before her wedding. Helpless and shocked, she watched her 'husband' sail away, without so much as a word of explanation. When her fatherless son grows up he sets off to sea, determined not to return to his New Brunswick home until he has sought vengeance on the man who treated his mother so heartlessly.
ISBN 10: 0-88780-570-1 ISBN 13: 978-0-88780-570-7

By Margaret Marshall Saunders
Beautiful Joe
Cruelly mutilated by his master, Beautiful Joe, a mongrel dog, is at death's door when he finds himself in the loving care of Laura Morris. A tale of tender devotion between dog and owner, this novel is the framework for the author's astute and timeless observations on farming methods, including animal care, and rural living. This Canadian classic,

written by a woman once acclaimed as "Canada's most revered writer," has been popular with readers, including young adults, for almost a century.
ISBN 10: 0-88780-540-X ISBN 13: 978-0-88780-540-X

Rose of Acadia
One hundred and fifty years have passed since the Acadians were sent into exile; now, Vesper Nimmo, a Bostonian, sets out for Nova Scotia's French shore with the intention of carrying out his great-grandfather's wish to make amends with the descendants of Agapit LeNoir. Nimmo finds himself immersed in the Acadians' struggles to preserve their culture and language and meets Rose à Charlitte, the innkeeper where he makes his temporary home. Their romance is thwarted by her past; but he cannot leave.
ISBN 10: 0-88780-571-X ISBN 13: 978-0-88780-571-4

By Frederick William Wallace
Captain Salvation
Captain Salvation is a little-known novel of Maritimers at sea, now brought back into print in this new addition to Formac's Fiction Treasures collection. It is an exciting tale of a young reprobate who works his way up from able seaman to mate, skipper and then a ship owner. His strength and intelligence pull him through the violent life aboard ship. Finally, shipwrecked off Cape Horn, he has to face his demons.
ISBN 10: 0-88780-676-7 ISBN 13: 978-0-88780-676-6

Blue Water
Set in the early 1900s, Blue Water traces the adventures of "Shorty" Westhaver from boyhood to young manhood in the dangerous and often tragic world of the Grand Banks fishery.
ISBN 10: 0-88780-709-7 ISBN 13: 978-0-88780-709-1

MEMBER OF SCABRINI GROUP

Québec, Canada
2006